MW01050316

EVADING
BABYLON

TIMES OF TURMOIL

BOOK ONE

EVADING
BABYLON

BY CHAD DAYBELL

spring creek
BOOK COMPANY
Provo, Utah

© 2012 Chad Daybell

All Rights Reserved.

This is a work of fiction and is not an official publication of The Church of Jesus Christ of Latter-day Saints. The characters, names, incidents, and dialogue are products of the author's imagination and are not to be construed as real.

ISBN 13: 978-1-932898-96-5
e. 1

Published by:
Spring Creek Book Company
P.O. Box 50355
Provo, Utah 84605-0355

www.springcreekbooks.com

Cover design © Spring Creek Book Company
Cover image © Mikhail Laptev | Dreamstime.com

Printed in the United States of America
Printed on acid-free paper

AUTHOR'S NOTE

In my previous series, *Standing in Holy Places*, I shared the experiences of three fictional families as they prepared for the Second Coming of Jesus Christ. The main purpose of that series was to give an overview of possible events we all might face in the coming years, and the novels covered several different story lines.

There were many times I wanted to slow down the pace and explore certain characters and scenes in greater detail, but I knew I needed to move forward with the overall series outline. Otherwise, the five-volume series could easily have expanded to ten or more volumes, and I wouldn't have completed it for several more years. I felt it was important to reach the series' finale in a reasonable time frame so readers could enjoy a satisfying conclusion.

With this new series I can now take readers back to the setting of *The Great Gathering*, the first volume in my previous series. In many ways, the global events described in that novel have already begun, and other key moments are fast approaching. The United States' economic situation has grown markedly worse since I wrote that book in 2006, and now I'm able to add many details that have emerged since that time.

Also, if you've read *The Great Gathering*, you'll notice similar scenes in this novel. This is because the same national events happen as they were portrayed in the previous series, but from the perspective of these new characters. In other words, both series take place in the same "universe" although the main characters from the two series don't interact with each other.

I want to emphasize that this is a work of fiction and the scenes involving Church leaders in particular are from my own imagination. I currently serve as my ward's Scoutmaster, and I certainly don't have any secret contacts or information concerning high-level meetings involving General Authorities. Those scenes are meant to move the storyline along and shouldn't be taken as factual. Besides, the novel is set in the future and those meetings wouldn't have taken place yet anyway.

I firmly believe the prophet's call for the Saints to gather to refuges of safety will come within a few years, but I don't feel that even the prophet yet knows the month or even the year it will happen. The call will likely come based on conditions in the United States, which aren't necessarily set in stone and can be altered based on the righteousness of the nation's citizens.

In this novel, the prophet's call for the Saints to gather together comes on a nice spring day, but in reality it might very well come in the middle of winter after a major snowstorm. The Lord has tested the faith of his Saints throughout history, and this might be another one of those times. I'm hoping for a sunny day, though.

Unlike the *Standing in Holy Places* series, which was structured around major prophesied events and had a pre-determined number of volumes, this one is more open-ended. I don't know how many volumes there will be in this series, and in many ways the story lines will be shaped by the events taking place around us. I suppose I will continue to write until the major events in the novels start becoming reality!

Thank you in particular to my wife Tammy and my children, as well as everyone who has given me encouragement and support over the years. I truly appreciate it!

Chad Daybell
May 2012

THE TURMOIL DEEPENS

As this story begins, the United States' position in the world has begun to falter.

"The Great Recession" that first battered the financial markets in 2008 created long-lasting effects, leading to a feeling of national unease as the unemployment rate remained stubbornly high. It was a daunting task for companies to add new jobs as the economy limped along, despite continual claims from the federal government that things were on the upswing.

Despite promises from Congress to trim the federal budget, the nation's leaders continued to pile up more than $1 trillion in additional debt each year. Even the most-optimistic analysts forecasted an economic tsunami unless immediate and drastic changes were made, but their pleas went unheeded.

Despite this massive debt looming over the nation, Congress could not agree on where to tighten the budget. Entitlement programs and interest payments were eating up a growing portion of the nation's expenditures, but the number of handouts to unemployed citizens continued to expand. These programs greatly reduced any incentive for these people to find jobs, leading to a sharp increase in the number of citizens who were essentially living off the government.

Then in the fall of 2011, a movement emerged to capitalize on the nation's uneasiness by organizing protests against the wealthy. It began when a group attempted to shut down New York City's financial sector, and their effort to "Occupy Wall Street" became a catch phrase, with similar protests sprouting up in other cities.

These blockades took on a darker tone in the summer of 2012, and from that point on the clash between the establishment and the so-called "99 percent" became more polarized and violent. The contentious U.S. presidential and congressional campaigns that year added to the nation's troubles, leading to outbreaks of civil unrest at levels that hadn't been seen since the 1960s.

Also, for several years the executive branch of the federal government had been quietly issuing mandates and executive orders that slowly but surely eroded the Christian foundation of America. Religious institutions faced fines or other penalties if they didn't comply with edicts that were blatantly against their core beliefs. Congress and the judicial system failed to take serious action against these new policies, and in many ways the U.S. Constitution was indeed hanging by a thread.

On the global front, America's leaders seemed to ignore the growing overall strength of China, the renewed military power of Russia, and the danger posed by a volatile Iran. It was clear to many observers that there was a growing collaboration among these nations, but America's leaders seemingly turned a blind eye. Instead, they made substantial cutbacks in the U.S. military budget, weakening the country's defenses and leaving it more vulnerable to a possible attack.

Meanwhile, the world waited in anticipation for the Mayan Calendar to end on December 21, 2012—then everyone moved forward with their lives when the earth just kept on turning.

During this time, members of The Church of Jesus Christ of Latter-day Saints were warned and cautioned by their leaders in each General Conference to prepare themselves and their families for tougher times ahead. The importance of being both spiritually and temporally prepared was clearly emphasized.

The prophets recognized that important events that had been prophesied for generations were now coming to fruition, and the spiritual commitment of each Church member would be tested to the limit during this time of sifting and refinement. Those who stood faithful during these darkest hours would emerge triumphantly into a glorious era when the wicked would be vanquished and New Jerusalem would be built.

But we're getting ahead of ourselves. We're only at the beginning of that story, where you'll meet Nathan Foster and Marie Shaw, two Latter-day Saints who are facing the same daily challenges you are. They and their family members might remind you of people in your ward or neighborhood. Here's their story.

CHAPTER 1

On a brisk February morning, more than a thousand Latter-day Saints were gathered together for a stake conference in Minneapolis, Minnesota to hear the words of Elder Smith of the Quorum of Twelve Apostles.

"The meeting might actually end on time," Elder Nathan Foster whispered to his companion Elder Graham as he pointed to his watch. They were sitting on folding chairs with a few other missionaries in the meetinghouse foyer as Elder Smith addressed the congregation.

Despite a heavy snow overnight, Elder Smith's presence at the conference had generated a huge turnout. In addition to the multitude of active members in attendance, dozens of less-active families had come to see the apostle, completely filling the chapel, cultural hall, and stage, and flowing out into the foyer where the missionaries were.

Nathan refocused on Elder Smith's words, who said, "The members of the Church will soon face some life-changing decisions. We'll all encounter a variety of difficulties as the Second Coming approaches, but the key is to obey the prophet no matter what comes our way. Those Saints who disregard his words will find themselves in both physical and spiritual peril."

The apostle's comments caused Nathan to think briefly about his own future. It was pretty much up in the air. The only sure thing was that he would be released from the Minnesota Minneapolis Mission in 16 days—not that he was counting.

Elder Smith ended his remarks right on time, and following

the closing hymn, everyone bowed their heads for the benediction. Nathan began to close his eyes, but something unusual caught his attention. A classroom door had quietly opened and a clean-cut, well-dressed man marched purposely up the hallway, heading for the chapel doors.

"*Stop him,*" the Spirit whispered to Nathan, who hesitated for a moment before standing up to block the man's path. Nathan noticed the man was holding what looked like a scripture case, but it bulged in the middle and didn't look right.

"I can't let you into the chapel," Nathan told the man as they came face to face.

"Hey, watch out," the man said, trying to elbow past the missionary. Nathan swatted at the man's hand, knocking the scripture case to the floor. The man lunged forward to retrieve it, but then a high-pitched beep emitted from the case.

"No!" the man cried before recoiling in fear and scrambling back down the hallway.

"Don't let him get away!" Nathan shouted at two men standing in the hall. They stopped the man as Nathan picked up the case and raced through the foyer's double doors. As he got outside, he spotted a big pile of snow at the end of the shoveled sidewalk and threw the case in that direction.

BOOM!

The case exploded just as it reached the snow, obliterating the pile and creating a five-foot-wide smoking crater of rocks and soil. Nathan was jolted backward by the blast and pelted by debris. He landed hard on his right shoulder on the icy sidewalk, and something inside him cracked. The pain was intense, and he slipped into unconsciousness.

The explosion shattered all of the windows on that side of the meetinghouse, cutting short the closing prayer. Shards of glass rained down on members of the congregation, and cries of pain and dismay erupted inside the chapel. Elder Smith was instantly surrounded on the stand by his security team and escorted out the far side of the building into a waiting car that whisked him away to safety. In all of the commotion, Nathan lay unnoticed on the sidewalk for nearly a minute until Elder Graham rushed outside to find him.

"Elder Foster, are you all right?" he cried, shaking his companion's shoulder.

Nathan slowly opened his eyes, not immediately remembering what had happened. He touched his ribs and moaned, "Ouch, that really hurts. Hey, how come I'm outside?"

"You saved the day!" Elder Graham said. "You grabbed that bomb and threw it outside before it went off."

Nathan suddenly remembered the confrontation with the man in the foyer. "Did they catch the guy?"

"Yes," Elder Graham said. "They've got him pinned in a classroom right now."

"That's a relief," Nathan said.

❧

Several ambulances soon arrived to care for the injured Saints, and Nathan was taken to a nearby hospital. The medical tests and X-rays showed some cracked ribs, a few cuts, and a badly bruised shoulder, but there weren't signs of major damage. Elder Graham had given him a priesthood blessing in the ambulance and had stayed at his side throughout the ordeal. By the time their mission president arrived that afternoon, Nathan was feeling a lot better.

"Hello, President Warren," Nathan said, grasping his leader's hand. "You didn't have to come . . ."

President Warren smiled. "It's an honor. Thank you for saving a lot of lives. It's a miracle that none of the other missionaries were hurt."

Nathan shook his head. "I didn't even have time to think before I grabbed the package. Wait, I wouldn't say that. The Spirit told me to stop the man."

Nathan explained how he'd received the prompting, and the president nodded. "You've told me before how the Spirit has guided you throughout your mission, so I'm not surprised you responded so quickly."

A medical attendant stuck his head in the room and said, "Turn on the TV news. They're going to talk about what happened."

President Warren grabbed the remote and clicked on the room's TV. "It should be interesting to see how the local media covers the story," he said.

A stern-faced anchorman appeared on the screen with the caption "*Breaking Story: Mormon Bombing*" appearing below him.

The president frowned. "Judging from that, I'm not sure if that means we were the bomber or the target!"

The anchorman stared into the camera and said, "A major catastrophe was averted this morning at a Mormon church in Minneapolis, but there was still severe damage and many injuries reported. Let's go to the scene."

The broadcast switched to a female reporter standing in the snow outside the meetinghouse. The church's shattered windows were visible and the camera briefly zoomed in on the crater in the lawn, which was now cordoned off by yellow police tape.

"According to eyewitnesses, a high-ranking Mormon Church leader was speaking here this morning to a large crowd," the reporter said. "As the meeting ended, a man rushed toward the leader with a bomb, but a quick-thinking church missionary intercepted the man and tossed the bomb outside just as it detonated. As you can see, there was a lot of damage, including the shattering of several car windows in the parking lot, but it could have been much worse."

The reporter motioned toward the meetinghouse and added, "About twenty members of the congregation were taken to local hospitals with cuts from the shattered windows, but it appears everyone will recover."

"That's good news," the anchorman said as the broadcast shifted to a split-screen. "Did they catch the suspect?"

"Yes," the reporter said. "He's been identified as Kurt Jessop, a disgruntled ex-Mormon. He's in police custody at this time."

"Tell us about the true hero in this story—the young man who got the bomb out of the building," the anchorman said. "How's he doing?"

"Church leaders say he's a full-time Mormon missionary from Utah named Nathan Foster. He was injured in the blast and taken to a local hospital, so we haven't been able to talk to him yet, but we'll give you more details as they become available."

"Thank you for that report. In other news . . ."

President Warren clicked off the TV and smiled at Nathan. "Yes, you're indeed a hero."

CHAPTER 2

Nathan enjoyed talking with President Warren and Elder Graham for another few minutes, but he could hardly keep his eyes open.

"We better let Elder Foster recuperate," President Warren told the nurse. "I think he's ready for a long night's sleep."

She agreed. "I know these guys usually stay in pairs, but we've got him covered."

"Are you sure?" Elder Graham asked. "I'm willing to stay the night at his bedside."

President Warren looked at the nurse. "We'll still be able to have Church security posted outside his door, right?"

"Yes. We won't let anyone in without your approval."

"Very good," he said before turning to Elder Graham. "Come enjoy a nice meal and a good night's sleep at the mission home."

Elder Graham looked unsure, but Nathan said, "I'll be fine," before giving his companion a farewell wave.

The nurse checked his charts, then turned out his light. Within a few minutes he was asleep, but he soon awoke from a dream in which Elder Smith had been killed because Nathan hadn't stopped the bomber. The dream was very vivid and left him shaking.

Nathan prayed fervently that he could have a peaceful night's sleep, and once again he drifted off into another dream. This one was also very vivid, but it had a much different feel to it. Nathan found himself standing in the center of a huge room with a towering ceiling. The walls appeared to sparkle like diamonds, and the floor was made of polished granite.

At the far end of the room Nathan could see the building's second and third floors. These floors were cordoned off with three-foot-high white railings that connected to a spiral staircase in each corner.

People began to fill the second floor, including many people he knew. Several of them looked over the railing and called out to him. Nathan waved to his former bishop, his father, and even to Marie Shaw, a girl his age who had befriended him as a teenager and helped him stay active in the Church.

Nathan also noticed the current members of the Quorum of the Twelve mingling among the people. They wore white suits and seemed to radiate goodness and purity. The people flocked around them and eagerly talked with them.

Then Nathan sensed people behind him, and he was surprised to have the three members of the LDS Church's First Presidency move next to him. They were also wearing white suits.

The prophet patted him on the shoulder and said, "These Saints of God have been faithful thus far, but a crucial time of decision has come. We've warned them enough. Let's see which way they choose to spiral."

"Spiral?" Nathan asked.

"You'll see," the prophet said.

Then the First Presidency took several steps forward before calling out to the group on the second floor. The people saw them and waved excitedly.

"Look! It's the prophet and his counselors," a woman cried out. "Let's listen to them."

When he had everyone's attention, the prophet raised his hands and gave the people a message. Nathan was now several feet behind the prophet and for some reason he couldn't hear what was being said, so Nathan watched the reactions of the people on the balcony.

To his surprise, most of the Saints seemed angry or alarmed by the prophet's words. These people turned to each other and expressed their dismay that the prophet would say such things.

As the prophet ended his message, he moved forward again and began climbing one of the spiral staircases. His counselors followed behind him, but as they reached the second level, they didn't stop to greet the people. Instead, they kept climbing up the spiral stairs until they reached the empty third level, where they leaned over the railing and motioned for the people below to follow them.

The members of the Quorum of the Twelve immediately went to the stairs and joined the First Presidency on the third level. Several other people followed them, but the vast majority stayed on the second floor.

Then things really got interesting. Nathan noticed his father essentially slide down the spiral banister to the first level, along with most of the people who had reacted angrily to the prophet's message.

Nathan focused on his former bishop, who danced from one foot to the other as if he couldn't decide which direction to go. He talked with his wife for a while before finally taking her hand and descending the spiral stairs to the first level.

Then Nathan located Marie Shaw. She had apparently started down the stairs to the first level, but her father had grabbed her by the arm and had pulled her back up to the second level.

They were in a heated argument, and neither one seemed willing to budge. Nathan was baffled by Marie's actions, but he noticed several other families having similar arguments. In some instances there were teenagers urging older relatives to climb upward, and in some cases there were older people fighting with each other.

The whole scene was confusing to Nathan, although he was starting to grasp that the arguments were symbolic of a greater struggle.

Suddenly Elder Smith of the Quorum of the Twelve called out to him from the top floor. "Elder Foster, soon the second level will be empty, because everyone must accept or reject the prophet's invitation. No one will be able to coast along in the middle anymore."

Nathan started to reply, but in an instant, he found himself back in his hospital bed. He looked around the room, stunned that the dream hadn't been real. He shielded his eyes from the morning sun that shined on his face through the room's window.

"That was weird, but it felt like a vision," he thought. "I better write it down."

Chapter 3

As Nathan's mind cleared from the strange dream, he sat up and hit the button next to the bed to page his nurse. When she arrived, he asked, "Could you please bring me a pen and a notepad?"

"You bet," she said. "Then in a few minutes I'll bring you breakfast."

Once she brought him the items, Nathan spent fifteen minutes writing down the details of what he called his "Spiral Dream" before the nurse returned with his food.

Nathan noticed a small American flag was planted in the center of his stack of pancakes. "What's this for?" he asked.

"It's Presidents Day," she said. "Sorry you have to spend it in the hospital."

Nathan put the flag next to his scriptures and quickly ate the pancakes. As he finished eating, the nurse returned once again.

"A special visitor has requested to see you," she said. "Do you feel strong enough to visit with him?"

"Who is it?" Nathan asked. "President Warren told me not to talk to any reporters without him here."

"Don't worry. This man has already been approved by President Warren," she said, pointing to someone in the hall. Nathan looked past her and saw Elder Smith standing in the doorway with two security officers behind him.

"Come in!" Nathan said happily, motioning for the apostle to join him.

Elder Smith came to his bedside. "Are you feeling all right?"

"Yes, it's just a bump on the head. I'll be better in no time."

Elder Smith patted his shoulder. "I just wanted to thank for what you did. I would've visited you yesterday, but everything around here turned into a circus."

"I know what you mean," Nathan said. "I'm just glad I was in the right place at the right time. The Spirit prompted me to confront that guy, so I did."

Elder Smith nodded. "I'm glad you responded so quickly. We've had our eye on Kurt Jessop for a while. This isn't his first confrontation with me, but it's certainly the worst."

Nathan looked up in surprise. "You've met him before?"

"When I was serving as his stake president a few years ago, Kurt was excommunicated. There were a long list of reasons why it needed to happen, but he wouldn't take responsibility for his actions. I know he still blames me, although I was just doing what was required. As often happens with former members of the Church, he now devotes his time and energy fighting against us. Kurt told the police last night that when he heard I'd be speaking here, his anger boiled over and he planned the bombing."

"That's terrible," Nathan said. "You don't deserve that kind of treatment."

"It comes with the calling," Elder Smith said. "As you know, the Church is coming under increased pressure across the nation to support gay marriage and other such issues, but I assure you we won't change our stance. The Plan of Salvation has been in operation throughout the eternities, and we aren't going to adjust our doctrines simply because of political pressure."

"That's what we've told people here when they confront us about those things," Nathan said. "It seems like they're more mean-spirited than when I started my mission, and the opposition appears to be growing."

"That's been the trend across the nation for our missionaries," Elder Smith said. "Safety is becoming an issue in some areas."

Elder Smith waved his hand and said, "Enough about that, right? I came here to thank you for not only saving my life, but also to get to know you a little better. So please tell me a bit about yourself. I talked to President Warren last night, and he said you've served an outstanding mission."

Nathan was happy to hear that. He'd only had a few baptisms during his mission, but he felt he'd made a real difference in reactivating many of the members.

Nathan shrugged. "Well, the fact I'm even on a mission is kind of a miracle in itself."

"What do you mean?" Elder Smith asked.

Nathan took a deep breath. "I didn't have the best upbringing. Dad had an affair when I was eight years old, and my parents got divorced. Then Mom was diagnosed with thyroid cancer when I was 14, and although she fought hard against it for a few years, she died a few months into my mission."

"I'm sorry," Elder Smith said. "How did your siblings handle everything?"

"Well, I was an only child, but I have a 12-year-old half-sister, because Dad eventually married the woman he had the affair with."

"Are you close to them?"

"Not at all," Nathan said. "I only saw Dad a few times after the divorce. He would stop by our house, but I was so angry with him that the visits were horrible for both of us. Mom finally said I didn't need to see him anymore. Dad seemed fine with the arrangement, so I've never even met his wife or my sister."

"That must have been challenging," Elder Smith said.

Nathan wiped his eyes. "Yes. I'd held onto some hard feelings toward Dad, but early in my mission I reached the conclusion I needed to forgive him or it would eat me up inside. So I have."

"Very good," the apostle said. "So with everything that was going on in your life, how did you develop a testimony?"

Nathan smiled sheepishly. "Well, I owe most of my initial motivation to attend Church to Marie Shaw, a girl who was in our ward as I grew up. She was pretty and was always nice to me, plus she made comments like, 'See you next week, Nathan.'"

"Thank goodness for righteous young women," Elder Smith

said with a grin. "But is Marie the basis of your testimony?"

"Absolutely not," Nathan said. "In fact, Marie eventually went to college at the University of Utah and I haven't seen her since our high school graduation. By the end of high school I'd read the Book of Mormon and had received an answer that it was true. Then I started attending Institute classes at Utah Valley University, and I gained the conviction that I needed to serve a mission."

"Excellent," Elder Smith said. "What are your future plans? Is there a young lady like Marie waiting patiently for your return?"

Nathan chuckled. "Hardly. My plan is to do landscaping work this coming summer to earn tuition money, then attend UVU in the fall. Mom had to sell the house to pay for her cancer treatments, so it looks like I'll be living with her sister Susan in Salt Lake until I can find an apartment near campus. Nothing is set in stone, though."

Nathan then paused and looked at the notepad he had set aside. He picked it up and said, "Elder Smith, last night I had a really unusual dream, and you were in it. So was Marie. It was almost like a vision, so I wrote it down this morning. Maybe it was caused by bumping my head, but I feel it really means something. Would you please read it?"

"Certainly," Elder Smith said. He took the notepad and intently read Nathan's notes about his dream. When he finished, he raised his eyebrows. "I assure you this is an inspired dream and has deep significance."

Nathan let out a sigh of relief. "I'm glad you don't think I've gone crazy."

Elder Smith shook his head. "Not at all."

The apostle then paused as if he were searching for the right words before saying, "Soon the Church is going to need hundreds of righteous young men such as yourself to fulfill key assignments in an important new project. We're looking for recently returned missionaries who have flexible schedules, and I think you'd be a perfect candidate."

"What would I be doing?" Nathan asked.

"Well, in some respects this assignment would still feel like a mission, but the Church would provide housing and cover other expenses. In essence, it would be a full-time job with all of your needs taken care of."

"I could handle that," Nathan said eagerly. "When will this project begin?"

"We don't really know yet," Elder Smith said. "It might not be for a few months, but once you get home and settled in, contact my office in Salt Lake. We'll have more details by then."

"That sounds great," Nathan said. "I've had a couple of companions who might be interested as well."

The apostle frowned. "I would keep this topic confidential for now. I wouldn't even discuss it with other missionaries, because only 'the best of the best' will receive this invitation. I admit the job could end up being a bit rigorous at times, but it will be worthwhile to you."

Nathan suddenly felt a tinge of self-doubt. "Maybe I wouldn't be cut out for this assignment . . ."

Elder Smith held up his hand. "Your prompt response yesterday in heeding the Spirit showed me you've got what it takes, and this dream is an indication that the Lord feels the same way. Keep that dream fresh in your mind, because I believe you'll soon see it fulfilled."

"Then what do you think the dream means?" Nathan asked.

Elder Smith smiled slightly and rubbed his chin. "Well, there's a lot of symbolism in it, but I feel the main message is that the time is coming quickly when the Lord will expect more from his Saints. This will cause a division to emerge in the Church. Some will continue to follow the prophet, while others will decide it isn't worth the effort."

Nathan nodded. "It's kind of like in the Bible when the Savior invited his followers during one of his sermons to step it up a notch, but most of the people didn't want to be bothered."

"Exactly. The whole purpose of the project I mentioned is to help the members of the Church become better Saints."

Nathan smiled. "That sounds like something I would love to be a part of."

"I know you would," Elder Smith said. "So go ahead and return to Utah, and get settled back into life. But if you're still interested in a few weeks, then call my secretary at Church headquarters in Salt Lake and tell her I had recommended that you work in the MM Program. She'll transfer you to the right department."

Elder Smith then took out a card with his secretary's phone number on it and wrote "MM Program" on the back before handing it to Nathan.

"What does MM stand for?"

"You'll find out soon enough," Elder Smith said. "Don't worry, everything will work out according to the Lord's timetable."

CHAPTER 4

That same afternoon, Marie Shaw was driving southbound on Interstate 15 heading to her parents' home in Orem, Utah. Her semester at the University of Utah had been stressful, and since she didn't have classes because of Presidents Day, she'd decided to visit her parents rather than sit around in her campus apartment.

It was an unusually warm day, and Marie definitely had a case of "Spring Fever." She pulled her long brown hair back into a ponytail and rolled the windows down on her Volkswagen Jetta. The car stereo was tuned to a pop-rock station, and she started singing along to popstar Britney Spears' recent hit, "Till the World Ends."

Marie laughed to herself, thinking about the song's basic message of focusing on worldly pleasures rather than worrying about the future. Instead, Britney encouraged everyone to just go to a nightclub and "keep on dancing till the world ends."

"You go for it, Britney," Marie said, "but I don't think life's always going to be that easy."

As the song ended, the radio DJ said, "We're getting more details about that thwarted bombing in Minnesota yesterday that targeted one of the Mormon apostles. Apparently the big hero was a missionary named Nathan Foster from Utah County. Reports say he confronted the bomber and then actually tossed the bomb outside, saving many lives. Way to go, Elder Foster!"

Marie nearly ran off the road when she heard the missionary's name. She and Nathan had been in the same ward growing up, and they had become good friends before she headed off to college.

Curiously, just a few days earlier she'd been wondering where he had ended up.

"I guess he's doing all right!" she told herself. Another song started playing, and Marie turned up the volume. The song had a catchy synthesizer rhythm and consisted of only a few words, but it was becoming a national sensation. The chorus was, "It's hip to get the chip, yeah, yeah. Do it right, and don't get left behind. It's hip to get the chip!"

Marie had read in *People* magazine that the song was actually written by the prolific songwriter and performer Lady Gaga, and Marie could definitely hear the artist's style in the music.

Marie started singing along, then she looked into the car next to her and noticed a burly male driver singing along as well. They both laughed and gave each other a thumbs-up sign before he sped off ahead of her.

When the song ended, the DJ said, "That's the new smash hit 'Get the Chip' by the group Chippy and Friends. It's a stupid name for a group, but that song is awesome!"

⤚

When Marie got to her parents' home, she was happy to find her mother Carol there.

"Wasn't that bombing in Minnesota terrible?" Carol asked as they sat around the kitchen table and munched on some freshly baked cookies. "I'm so grateful Elder Smith is okay."

Marie nodded. "On the radio just now they said the missionary is a Nathan Foster from Utah. Could it be the Nathan we know?"

"I would imagine," Carol said. "The local news is about to start. Go turn on the TV and see if they say anything."

As expected, the bombing was the lead story, with a spokesman from the LDS Church saying that about two dozen Saints were recovering from cuts and bruises from the chapel's shattered windows, but that everyone was going to recover.

Then the report shifted to the local angle, and Nathan Foster's senior yearbook photo was shown.

Marie smiled. "I was right! It's him."

The report explained that Nathan was currently still hospitalized but would be returning home from his mission in about two weeks. As the report concluded, Marie went to the computer and looked up additional stories about the bombing.

Carol let Marie browse the internet undisturbed, secretly pleased at Marie's interest in Nathan. She knew her daughter hadn't been attending church very often during her time at college, and it bothered her. Marie needed friends who were a bit more devoted to the gospel.

After a few minutes, Carol grabbed the plate of cookies and moved to Marie's side at the computer, where she was looking at a recent photo of Nathan that a Church member in Minnesota had posted on a blog.

"Hey, he's cuter than I remembered," Carol said. "Maybe you should give him a call when he gets home."

"Mom, we were just friends!" Marie said in feigned disgust, but she had already decided to attend his homecoming talk.

≈

As Nathan was resting in his hospital bed that evening, the president of the United States came on for a special primetime Presidents Day broadcast on all of the TV networks.

As a missionary, Nathan had been sheltered from everyday life, but he'd heard a lot of the propaganda about something called "the chip" for the past few weeks. In seemingly every conversation they'd had with people, the topic would always turn to the chip. It was being mentioned in mysterious commercials and even in a hit song he'd heard blaring from passing cars. Now it looked like the president was finally going to explain what it was. He began by holding up a small capsule that the camera zoomed in on.

"You are looking at a technological masterpiece," he said. "This tiny microchip can hold more information than a shelf full of books, and it is about to make all of our lives better."

He placed the chip in a tray on his desk and leaned earnestly toward the camera. "As a nation, we've all noticed a feeling of growing unrest for a variety of reasons. The civil disobedience is frightening, but this chip is the answer. I invite every U.S. citizen to receive their own personal chip. Your personal information will be loaded onto it, eliminating the need to carry ID cards or even credit cards. All transactions will be possible through the chip."

The president clasped his hands in front of him. "The purpose isn't to punish law-abiding citizens such as yourselves, but to stop those who are causing our distress. This chip would allow us to easily track those at scenes of violence and apprehend them. Also, it will essentially eliminate identity theft and protect our financial assets. Speaking of money, we will give a $2,000 tax credit to anyone who receives their chip by the end of February."

The president added, "As we celebrate this special holiday, I believe our noble presidents George Washington and Abraham Lincoln would have welcomed such an innovative technology if it had been available in their times."

The president then explained that "chip implant centers" had been established in all major cities. He emphasized that those who waited beyond the end of the month would have to pay an implantation fee and would lose the tax credit.

The president ended the broadcast by saying, "This program will boost our economy, reduce crime, and make our lives much more efficient. It is a 10-second procedure that only stings a little. I know, because I received the chip myself earlier today."

The president held up his right hand, and the camera zoomed in on it. He pointed to a tiny puncture on the back of his hand.

"See, it's hardly noticeable," he said. "As a nation, what have we got to lose?"

Nathan turned off the TV and rolled onto his side. The president's message had made him sick to his stomach. During the past two years of knocking on doors, he had met literally hundreds of families who depended on the government to pay all their bills for them. It wasn't that they were disabled and couldn't work—they were just happy to let Uncle Sam foot the bill. They weren't rich, but they could sit at home all day. To Nathan, the chip seemed like just another way for the government to shackle the people.

"Well, they'll have to give my $2,000 to someone else," he thought. "There's no way I'm getting that thing."

CHAPTER 5

Two weeks later, Nathan braced himself as his flight touched down at the Salt Lake International Airport. He was joined by Elder Grobben, a former companion who was also returning to Utah. Elder Grobben knew about Nathan's family situation, and he'd arranged with his parents to drop off Nathan at his Aunt Susan's home in Salt Lake, who was out of town until the next day.

The days since the bombing had flown by for Nathan. He'd thrown himself back into missionary work after being released from the hospital, although the only thing the people they visited wanted to talk about was how they were going to spend their "chip money." Despite that obstacle, Nathan had been privileged to baptize two investigators on his last Sunday in the mission field.

Now he felt a rush of emotions. He wasn't too excited to return home and face his family's troubles again. He had prayed nightly during his mission for his father to have a change of heart and return to the Church, but Nathan sensed the timing wasn't right—and might never be.

The two missionaries made their way to the airport's main entrance, where a large group was waiting to greet Elder Grobben. Cheers erupted as the group spotted the missionaries.

"I think they're happy to see you!" Nathan said. "I'll wait for you at the baggage area."

"Hey, stay with me," Elder Grobben said. "I'm sorry no one is here to greet you, but there are plenty of hugs to go around."

Elder Grobben was soon engulfed by his family members, but he stepped back and introduced Nathan to them. Elder Grobben's mom stepped forward and embraced him.

"Every missionary deserves a mom's hug when he gets home," she whispered in his ear, and Nathan felt tears come to his eyes.

"Thank you. That means a lot," he whispered back.

Soon they moved as a group to the baggage claim area. He picked up his two suitcases when he heard a familiar voice.

"Hello, son. You're looking good."

Nathan turned around in shock. His father Garrett stood nearby.

"Dad! What a surprise," Nathan said. "The Grobbens were going to drop me off at Aunt Susan's house . . ."

"I can do that if you want," Garrett said, watching Nathan's face. "Uh, this is all right, isn't it?"

"Sure, but I just didn't think you'd want—"

"Not want to pick up my son?" Garrett asked with a grin. "We've had our struggles, but I want to start fresh."

Nathan couldn't quite believe his eyes. His dad was clean-cut and seemed happier than he remembered.

Nathan quickly explained to Elder Grobben that he had a ride after all. "My dad is here to pick me up."

"Really?" Elder Grobben asked. "If you want, we can still take you—"

"No, this will be fine," Nathan said.

Elder Grobben shrugged. "Okay, but don't hesitate to call me if you need anything."

"I will. Thanks again."

Nathan turned back toward Garrett, who reached out to take one of the suitcases from his son. "I'm glad you're home," he said. "I'll still take you to Susan's house, but I'm hoping you'll agree to stay with us instead."

Nathan stammered, "I guess that would be okay. Have you talked with her about it?"

"Yes, and she thinks it would be a good idea. We've got a spare bedroom you can use. Vanessa and Denise are eager to get to know you . . . and so am I."

They soon loaded the luggage into Garrett's Honda Civic and got on I-80 heading east to reach I-15. Nathan noticed some landslides on the mountains above the University of Utah campus that had been caused by a substantial earthquake a few weeks before.

"I saw some footage of the earthquake at a member's house," Nathan said. "Were you affected by it?"

"Well, it snarled the freeway system for a while, but they've got things under control," Garrett said. "I'm just glad I wasn't living in some of those houses up on the bench. The people living on the fault line got the worst of it, although it shook the valley floor pretty good as well."

As they approached the freeway interchange, Nathan assumed they were going to the home in Bountiful where his father had moved after the divorce, but they got on I-15 heading south.

"Where are we going?" Nathan asked.

"Oh, I thought your mom would've told you. I moved back to Orem when she was diagnosed with cancer. I live about a block from our old house."

Nathan furrowed his brow. "Mom never mentioned it in her emails to me. I didn't know you two still talked."

"Well, I still paid your child support until you turned 18, and I always liked to hear how you were doing. I often asked her to let me visit with you, but she felt it was best if I stayed out of your life. I suppose I could've taken her to court over the visitation agreement, but I felt I'd already inflicted enough pain on her, so I followed her wishes. But now she is gone, I decided to take a chance . . ."

Nathan felt strange inside. It had never dawned on him that his father still cared about him. "I don't know what to say. I feel like I've lost a whole decade with you."

"Believe me, so do I, but what's done is done." Garrett's face displayed a brief flash of grief. "You probably don't know that I attended her funeral. I was hoping to see you there, but they said you had stayed on your mission. I admire you for that."

Nathan did a double-take. "You saw Mom's family?"

"Yes, and I even got a hug from Aunt Susan. It was awkward, but I needed the closure. Frankly, so did they."

"Wow. I thought they would've strung you up by your ankles right there in the church."

Garrett smiled. "Well, when Susan first saw me, she did give me a look that would've sent most people running. But hopefully time can heal all wounds, including the ones I caused you. Son, I'm truly sorry."

Nathan was silent for nearly a minute, his mind swimming. He finally asked, "Do you regret what you did?"

Garrett gave him a sideways glance. "The affair? Yes, it was a huge mistake, and you and your mom didn't deserve it. But I'm happy I have Vanessa and Denise in my life. You'll like them."

Nathan felt the answer was a bit hollow. "That's it? You put me and Mom through an emotional hurricane! It's a miracle I turned out halfway normal. What about the Church? Where do you stand?"

"I'm still excommunicated, if that's what you mean," Garrett said with a sigh. "But I don't hold any hard feelings against the Church. I deserved what I got."

"Do you still believe the gospel?"

Garrett stared straight ahead. "My issue was never with the doctrine. So I do believe it, but right now I wouldn't consider rejoining. Vanessa is a devoted Catholic, and she takes Denise to church each week. I'm content with that. But enough about me. Tell me about your mission."

Nathan was happy to change the subject, and once he got talking, he couldn't stop telling his father about the various experiences he'd had in Minnesota, including saving Elder Smith from the bomber.

"Yes, I followed the whole thing through the Minnesota media websites," Garrett said.

"Really?"

"Of course! You're my son. I nearly called you when they reported you were in the hospital, but when it was clear you'd recover, I decided it would be best to surprise you this way."

Nathan smiled. "A call from you would've been a shock to my system, that's for sure."

Garrett soon pulled off the freeway at the Orem Center Street exit and pulled into a gas station. Nathan watched as his dad held his right hand over a scanner at the pump, and suddenly the pump kicked on. Garrett removed the gas cap, inserted the nozzle, and started filling the car without even touching a button. He then grabbed his cell phone while he waited and punched in a speed-dial number.

"Hi, honey," Garrett said. "Everything is going fine. Nathan and I should be there in about five minutes. Love you."

As Garrett got back in the car, Nathan said, "I noticed you used your chip. Did it hurt to get it?"

"Not at all, and it sure is convenient," Garrett said. "Are you going to get chipped?"

"Probably not," Nathan said. "The Church sent out a letter discouraging it."

"That's what I've heard, but it really has made my life so much easier. I don't even carry my wallet anymore."

They headed east and soon arrived in front of a nice home that was a couple of blocks south of Mountain View High School, Nathan's alma mater. They climbed out of the car and grabbed the suitcases.

"Vanessa and Denise are nervous to meet you, so please be kind," Garrett said.

"Don't worry," Nathan said. "I'll be a gentleman."

The front door opened, and a stunning Hispanic woman came outside, followed by her pre-teen look-alike.

"Sheesh, they're beautiful," Nathan muttered to Garrett. "How am I supposed to hold a grudge against them?"

Garrett smiled. "Maybe you shouldn't."

Vanessa came forward and shook Nathan's his hand. "I'm so happy to finally meet you. Welcome to our home."

"Thank you," Nathan said, surprised at the instant connection he had with the woman he'd despised for so many years.

Then he turned to Denise. "You must be my little sister! How are you?"

Denise didn't say anything, but instead threw her arms around Nathan and started crying.

"She's happy you're here," Vanessa said softly, patting her daughter's head.

Denise soon backed away and said, "I'm sorry. I've just never had a brother before."

Everyone laughed, and they headed into the house where Vanessa and Denise had prepared a nice dinner. As they ate and chatted, Nathan truly felt loved and accepted.

❧

Nathan had previously arranged to meet with his stake president that night to be officially released as a missionary, so Garrett let Nathan take the car to do that. After a pleasant interview with the stake president, Nathan stopped by his bishop's house.

"You look great," Bishop Tanner said. "I'm relieved you weren't hurt worse in the bombing."

"Me too," Nathan said. "The Lord was watching over me."

"You got my latest letter, right?" the bishop asked. "Is Sunday still going to work for you to speak in Sacrament Meeting?"

"Yep, I'm planning on it."

After his visit with the bishop, Nathan decided to take a little journey around the old neighborhood, including a slow drive past his old home. The new occupants had painted it a bright color, and it didn't even seem like the same house.

He then drove to Marie Shaw's home. Her rebellious actions in his "spiral dream" remained vivid in his mind, and he still had a hard time believing it could be true.

"At least they haven't moved," he said as he recognized her father's car in the driveway. The lights were on in the front room, and Nathan surprised himself by pulling over to the curb.

"I just want to see how she's doing," he told himself. Then he realized he didn't have a reasonable excuse for why he was visiting her on his first evening back from his mission.

"You're such an idiot," he thought as he pulled back onto the road. "She surely has a boyfriend."

CHAPTER 6

Nathan felt like he was living in a whirlwind over the next few days. Since it wasn't landscaping season yet, Garrett had used his friendship with the local Toys-R-Us manager to get Nathan a night job there restocking shelves. They also went car shopping and found an affordable little blue Hyundai for him. Garrett made the first payment, but Nathan would take it from there.

Then suddenly it was Sunday morning and Nathan found himself sitting on the stand in the chapel getting ready to give his homecoming talk. He'd greeted many old friends before the meeting and it was great to be back in his old ward again. He'd been thrilled when Garrett, Vanessa, and Denise had surprised him the night before by saying they'd be at the meeting, and it was wonderful to see his dad receiving a warm welcome from several older members who had known him before the divorce.

As the opening song began, Nathan's heart jumped as he saw Marie and her parents enter the chapel and take a pew toward the front. As they settled in, Marie caught his eye and flashed him a big smile. He felt his face get red, and after a quick smile back, he concentrated on the words of the hymn.

As the Sacrament was passed to the congregation, Nathan kept his head down, praying that his talk would go well. His prayer was answered, and he gave a fine report that had the congregation captivated as he told of his experience in stopping the bomber. He concluded his talk by thanking the ward for helping his mother during her final days of suffering.

"It was hard to not come home for the funeral," Nathan said.

"That was a rough day for me, but I knew it was where I was supposed to be. Staying on my mission is what Mom would have wanted me to do." He paused to wipe away a tear before adding, "I felt her presence with me that day, and many times afterward. She's been watching over me."

After the meeting ended, Nathan was greeted by friends and family at the front of the chapel. Nathan saw Marie approaching and extended his hand toward her. She'd always been pretty in high school, but he couldn't help noticing she was now more attractive than he remembered.

"Marie! I'm so happy you came."

She took his hand. "Great talk, Nathan. I was impressed."

"Thank you. Who would've thought Minnesota could be so exciting?"

Marie laughed. "It sounds like you had more fun than I've had. It's pretty much been college classes for me ever since we last saw each other. I should graduate in December."

"Wow, now it's my turn to be impressed," Nathan said. "College looks like a long uphill trek for me right now."

Marie took a quick look around and saw several people still waiting to talk to Nathan.

"I better let you greet your other fans," she said with a wink. "My parents wanted to talk with you, but they team-teach the Gospel Doctrine class and had to go set things up. Would you like to come by our house tonight at about six for some pie and ice cream?"

"That sounds great," Nathan said. "Should I bring anything?"

"Nope! Just bring your cute smile."

Marie gave a quick wave, then slipped back into the crowd. Nathan felt a warm shiver travel down his spine. Had she actually been flirting with him?

CHAPTER 7

Nathan parked in front of Marie's house that evening and checked his hair in the rearview mirror. He'd tried not to read too much into his earlier conversation with her, but he had to admit he was hoping for the best.

He went to the front door, rang the bell, and was soon greeted by Marie's father.

"Hello, Brother Shaw," Nathan said.

"Hi, Nathan, and please just call me Aaron. That was a great talk today, by the way."

Aaron led Nathan into the kitchen, where Carol and Marie were checking on two pies that had just come out of the oven.

"It smells wonderful in here," Nathan said.

"We have pumpkin and apple," Marie said. "I couldn't remember which kind you liked."

Nathan shrugged. "How about some of both?"

Marie laughed, and soon they were seated at the kitchen table enjoying the pies and some vanilla ice cream.

"The ward hasn't changed too much while I was gone," Nathan said. "There were some younger couples I didn't recognize, but otherwise it looked like the same people."

"You're right, we've been pretty stable," Aaron said. "It sure was good to see your dad there, though. I talked to him for a minute before the meeting. You probably don't remember, but I worked with him in the Young Men presidency when you were little."

"I didn't know that! Yes, it was a relief when Dad told me he'd had a good experience today, and so did my stepmom and sister."

"Those two are beautiful," Carol said. "I've actually seen them once in a while in Wal-Mart, but I didn't know who they were."

"So are you going to live with your dad?" Marie asked.

"Yeah, it looks that way. My mom's sister Susan was going to let me live with her in Salt Lake, but Dad has welcomed me with open arms. It's been a little strange, to be honest, but so far it's been great. He's already helped me get a job and a car, so I can't complain."

"Where are you working?" Carol asked.

Nathan rolled his eyes. "I'm restocking shelves at Toys-R-Us each night after the store closes. It's fine, but I'm having a little trouble adjusting to the late hours. Brother Shaw—um, Aaron— are you still working at Novell?"

"Actually, I'm now at the National Security Agency's Data Center up near Camp Williams," Aaron said. "It's a longer drive, but the pay is much better. I'm enjoying it."

"That's good," Nathan told him. "Let me know if they need a daytime janitor!"

Aaron smiled. "I'll keep you in mind."

After a few more minutes of conversation, Carol and Aaron suddenly excused themselves, leaving Marie and Nathan alone at the table.

"I think they're hoping we'll get better acquainted," Marie said. "I'm nearly an old maid, you know! It seems like half of the people we graduated with are married already."

"I'm afraid it's going to be a while for me," Nathan said. "As you remember, I wasn't exactly a dating machine."

Marie shook her head. "You'll get back to UVU and have girls drooling over you."

Nathan laughed, then tried to change the subject by asking Marie about several of the kids they had grown up with. She finally grabbed their senior yearbook and sat next to him at the table. She knew what most of their peers were doing, and they talked for several more minutes before she added, "Of course, I'm kind of the black sheep of the group."

"What do you mean?" Nathan asked.

Marie rolled her eyes and said softly, "Mom thinks I've gone apostate or something because I haven't been going to church much. I admit I've slacked off, but none of my roommates are religious, and it's been easy to just sleep in on Sunday. Then I've been too busy to attend any Singles Ward activities."

Nathan was surprised, but he kept the conversation upbeat. "Hmm. So you're saying that the shining beacon of my teenage years has faded and is now an inactive spinster?"

Marie's jaw dropped, then she gave him a playful punch in the arm. "I knew you'd take Mom's side!"

Nathan grabbed her fist as she took another swing and twisted it a little. "Don't worry. I know how amazing you are."

Marie was genuinely touched by his words. "Thank you, Nathan. I've really missed your friendship."

"Well, you know where to find me. I'll be at Toys-R-Us each night starting at nine o'clock!"

His comment made her look at the clock. "Oh, I need to get back to my apartment tonight and print off a research paper. Sorry to cut this short."

"No problem at all. Please tell your parents how much I enjoyed the pies and ice cream."

Marie grabbed a paper from off the counter and wrote down her cell phone number. "Give me a call sometime. Maybe you could come up to Salt Lake and we could do lunch."

Nathan smiled. "That would be great."

CHAPTER 8

Nathan held off calling Marie on Monday, but by Tuesday he just wanted to hear her voice. As he searched his wallet for the paper with her phone number, he came across the business card with the contact information for Elder Smith's secretary.

"Maybe I can kill two birds with one stone," he said, turning the card over and seeing the words "MM Project." If he timed things right, maybe he could check into the Church job and then meet Marie for lunch. He figured any job the Church had in mind for him couldn't be worse than spending the wee hours of each morning unloading boxes of toys and sticking them on shelves. He was grateful for the job, since so many people were having a hard time finding work, but he couldn't see himself surviving this schedule once he was in college.

When he called Elder Smith's office, he spoke to the secretary and told her he was calling about the MM Project.

"Just one moment," she said. "Let me transfer you."

Nathan waited as another number began to ring. Soon a man answered by simply saying, "MM Project. How may I help you?"

"My name is Nathan Foster, and Elder Smith of the Quorum of the Twelve felt I would be a good fit for . . . for whatever this project is."

The man chuckled. "If Elder Smith told you to call, then I'm sure he was right. Would you be able to meet with me tomorrow at 11 a.m. for a preliminary interview?"

"Yes, that would be fine," Nathan said. "Do I need to bring anything, such as a resume?"

"No, just arrive on time and look presentable. If everything goes well, we'll give you more information at that time."

The man then gave Nathan the room number in the Joseph Smith Memorial Building where they would meet.

"Thank you for this opportunity," Nathan said.

"I think you'll find this to be the best job you've ever had," the man said. "When you arrive, just knock on the door and step inside."

Nathan said good-bye, then immediately called Marie.

"Hey, I'll be in Salt Lake tomorrow," he said. "Would you be able to go to lunch?"

"Yeah, I'd like that," she said. "Could you pick me up at my apartment at noon?"

"That will work for me."

Marie gave him the directions and then they chatted for a few minutes. After the call, Nathan felt like he was floating on air the rest of the day.

❧

The next morning Nathan nervously approached the door in the Joseph Smith Building. He did as he was told, knocking on the door and then opening it. He saw an older gentleman dressed in a suit sitting at a table. Nathan recognized him as Elder Wilford Miller of the First Quorum of the Seventy, a stocky man with brownish-gray hair and a quick smile.

"Hello, Nathan," he said as he stood to greet him. "I'm Elder Miller. It's a pleasure to meet you. I'm the one you spoke with yesterday on the phone."

"I thought I recognized your voice," Nathan said, feeling a bit more comfortable.

Elder Miller motioned for Nathan to take a seat across from him, then said, "After our conversation yesterday, I contacted Elder Smith, and he mentioned that you're the one who saved his life in Minnesota."

"Yes, that was me. I was just following the Spirit."

Elder Miller nodded. "That's a great trait to have."

Elder Miller then took a few minutes getting to know Nathan, and he seemed pleased with the responses. Finally the General Authority flipped through some papers in front of him, and slid one over to Nathan. It was his Church membership summary.

"Please look this over and see that we have everything in order," Elder Miller said. "I feel you're a great candidate for the job."

Nathan noticed his contact information needed to be changed to list his father's home address, and Elder Miller wrote that down. Once he was done, Nathan said, "I'm really interested in the job, but what exactly is this MM Project?"

"Well, it involves a lot of blue-collar labor, such as lifting and transporting things—but it isn't overly strenuous. It could also involve some security duty, such as patrolling Church property."

"I think I could handle that," Nathan said. "If you don't mind me asking, how much is the pay?"

"That's a fair question," Elder Miller said. "I'm sure you've heard of the Law of Consecration."

"Yes, I've studied about it."

"Then you know that the time is coming when the Lord will ask the Saints to consecrate everything they own to the building up of the Kingdom of God—including their time, talents, and possessions. As part of this assignment, you'll be asked to do that. You won't receive a salary, but the Church will cover all of your expenses and anything else you might need."

Nathan raised his eyebrows. "You mean, food, clothes . . ."

"Everything."

Nathan paused, a bit surprised at the answer. "How would I pay for college without a paycheck?"

"If you take this job, you'll have to postpone college. This will be a full-time commitment."

"How long would the job last?" Nathan asked.

Elder Miller rubbed his chin. "At least a year, but probably longer than that. Along those lines, your duties would likely take you away from your family and friends for extended periods of time. Would that be an issue?"

"Not really," Nathan said. "As I mentioned, Mom has passed away, and Dad and I aren't really too close. There's a girl I'm quite interested in, though."

Elder Miller cocked his head slightly. "Are you really attached to her?"

"I think I'm more attached to her than she is to me."

Elder Miller nodded. "I'm just saying that this job wouldn't allow you to see her very often, at least for several months. So take that into consideration. Anyway, certainly pray about the decision, but I think you're a perfect fit, and I'm hoping you'll accept it."

"I'm definitely leaning toward it," Nathan said. "Once I decide, how will I let you know?"

"If you choose to take the job, return to this room on Friday at 9 a.m., when we will be instructing several new trainees at once. If you don't want the job, just call Elder Smith's secretary again and tell her. She'll pass the word along to me. Otherwise, we'll see you on Friday morning!"

Elder Miller stood up, and they shook hands. Nathan left the interview feeling a bit confused, but in general he felt good about the chance to work for the Church.

CHAPTER 9

Nathan walked out of the Joseph Smith Memorial Building and checked his watch. He'd have to hurry if he wanted to reach Marie's apartment by noon. He went to his car and drove up the hill toward the University of Utah. Thankfully she had given him good directions, and promptly at noon he knocked on her front door. Soon the door opened.

"Hi, Nathan," Marie said. "You're right on time."

He took a deep breath. "Yeah, I had to jog from the parking lot to make it. I'm not as in shape as I thought I was."

"You look good to me," Marie said with a smile.

Her comment briefly flustered Nathan, but he said, "Well, where's a good place to eat around here?"

"I thought we'd go to a fun little sandwich place about two blocks away. Would that be all right?"

"Sounds great."

They left the apartment, and Marie took hold of his arm as they walked along and chatted. He was happy with that, but he was also surprised by her outfit. It was a pleasant March day, but her low-cut blouse revealed a little too much, and her skirt was well above her knees. In all of their teenage years together, he couldn't remember her dressing that way.

"You never told me exactly why you came to Salt Lake today," Marie said, pulling him closer.

"I actually had a job interview," Nathan said.

"Oh? Which company is hiring?" Marie asked. "I've got a couple of friends looking for work."

41

"It's with the Church. It would mainly be transporting stuff and doing some security duty."

"That sounds better than Toys-R-Us," Marie said. "Would you work here in Salt Lake?"

"They didn't give me many details, but I think so," Nathan said. "There's another meeting on Friday where I'll learn a lot more about it."

They arrived at the sandwich shop, and as they sat down at a table Nathan couldn't help noticing that Marie's skirt barely covered her upper thigh. She looked fit and trim, but the display of skin bothered him. Marie caught his eye and then shifted enough to pull her skirt down a little.

"Sorry about that," she said. "I'm not used to hanging out with a returned missionary. It's just such a nice day, and I wanted to wear something . . ."

"Don't worry about it," Nathan said, shifting his eyes to the menu. "Which sandwich would you recommend?"

❧

When they got back to the apartment, Marie's roommate Sheridan was there. She was a perky blonde girl dressed similarly to Marie.

"So you're the missionary man that Marie keeps talking about," Sheridan said with a smile. "She was right. You *are* cute."

Nathan smiled nervously. "I'm not quite sure how to answer that."

The girls laughed, and Sheridan said, "Just accept it."

She then turned to Marie and said, "Hey, I picked up the mail, and I think something came that you've been waiting for! It's on the table."

Marie went into the kitchen and picked up a letter addressed to her. "It's from Naples & Austin! Do you think this could really be it?"

Sheridan nodded eagerly. "Open it! Open it!"

Nathan was clearly confused, so as Marie carefully opened the envelope, Sheridan quickly explained, "Marie has applied for several internships and already received a offer here in Salt Lake, but she was waiting to hear back from this company in Chicago."

Marie unfolded a sheet of paper and started reading it intently. Suddenly she tossed it in the air and shouted, "Yes! I got it!"

Sheridan and Marie clutched each other in excitement, then Marie collared Nathan, pulling him into a group hug accompanied by more joyful screaming. Marie finally backed away, wiping tears of joy from her eyes.

"Sorry about that, Nathan, but I just feel so happy and relieved that I was accepted," Marie said. "This internship means everything to me. Naples & Austin is one of the best public relations firms in the country."

Sheridan picked up the letter and read through it. "Wow, they'll not only pay you, but they'll also give you a place to live. That's incredible."

Sheridan handed the letter to Nathan, who read:

Dear Ms. Shaw,

It is our privilege to offer you a paid internship with Naples & Austin in our Chicago office, which is located in the renowned Bloomingdale's Building along the city's famous Magnificent Mile. We would also provide a studio apartment nearby for your use during the duration of your internship.

In our interview, you mentioned you would be able to come to Chicago as soon as possible and complete your spring semester classes online if needed. That is what we would prefer, due to the large number of projects we have coming up. We want you to begin working in early April if possible. Please contact me personally to accept the offer and to arrange your arrival date.

On a personal note, I greatly enjoyed our interview last month. You showed great poise, charisma, and spunk, which will take you a long way in this business. I know you realize the opportunities this internship will create for you, including possible full-time employment with our firm, so make the most of it!

Sincerely,
Gretchen Howell
Vice President
Naples & Austin

"Wow, that's exciting," Nathan said as he handed the letter to Marie. "You hadn't even mentioned this before."

"I didn't say anything because I didn't think I had a chance, but Gretchen and I really clicked during the interview. It's going to be awesome! Maybe you can come out to visit me this summer."

"Yeah, that would be fun," he said, feeling a little stunned by how this lunch date had evolved.

"Well, you're welcome to hang out here, but first I need to call my parents, and then call Gretchen to accept the internship."

"That's okay," Nathan said. "I work tonight, so maybe I should head back to Orem. I'll talk to you soon."

He gave Marie a quick hug, and then shook hands with Sheridan as he departed. As he walked back to his car, he pondered the strange twist of events that had occurred in the past two hours. First he got a job offer he thought would bring him closer to Marie, and now suddenly it looked like she was going to be living in Chicago for several months.

He sensed if he took the Church job, it was unlikely he would ever be able to visit her in Chicago. Then there was Marie herself. She was more attractive than ever and she always made his heart beat faster when they were together, but something had clearly changed in her spiritual life.

Nathan reached his car and sat quietly behind the wheel.

"Heavenly Father, what is going on?" Nathan asked. "Please give me some guidance."

An image from the Spiral Dream he'd had in the Minnesota hospital came into his mind, particularly the part where he'd focused on Marie. He was astonished to realize that in the dream she had on the same clothing she'd been wearing that day. Nathan sensed there was a genuine conflict going on behind the smiles that Marie and her parents had been showing him.

"*Talk to her parents,*" the Spirit whispered.

Nathan nodded and started the engine, hoping to be able to catch Marie's parents home that evening.

After arriving home, he called the Shaws' number, but there wasn't an answer. He loaded the dishwasher after dinner, much to Vanessa's delight, then decided to just stop by their home.

Aaron answered the door and invited Nathan in. "How can I help you?" he asked. "Weren't you with Marie this afternoon? She said you were there when she opened her letter."

"Yes, I was," Nathan said. "I just wanted to talk to you and Sister Shaw, if that's all right."

"That's fine, but Carol isn't here," Aaron said. "Gary Pratt died, so she and the rest of the Relief Society presidency are meeting with the family to help arrange the funeral. But come have a seat in the living room. She should be back in a few minutes."

Nathan took a seat on the couch, and Aaron settled into a recliner.

"So Gary Pratt died? That's a surprise. He was a great example to me when he was my priest advisor."

Aaron shook his head sadly. "He'll surely be missed. It's surprising how many faithful older people have been passing away the past couple of weeks in our area. The newspaper's obituary section has been overflowing. It's as if the Lord is saying, "Well done. Now come home and help us on this side of the veil.""

"That makes sense," Nathan said. "Maybe the Lord is sparing them from the troubles that await us as times get tougher."

"I like that theory," Aaron said. "Believe me, from what I see at work, we're heading for some challenges."

"What do you mean?" Nathan asked.

A brief wave of nervousness passed over Aaron's face. "I shouldn't really say anything, but since I started working at the NSA Data Center my eyes have really been opened on how quickly this country has changed for the worse."

"In what ways? Are you talking about the chip?"

"Yes, but the chip is really just part of a national mindset that has evolved over the past few years. I've known the chip was coming for several months, and I honestly expected a public outcry against it. The public never would have accepted such an invasion of privacy in the 1980s or even at the time of 9/11, but I think we've gradually become accustomed to everyone knowing everyone else's business."

"I know what you mean," Nathan said. "I set up a Facebook account a few days ago to stay in touch with my mission friends, and I started adding friends from high school. I was shocked by what some of them were posting. I haven't seen them in three years, but I already know more about them than I ever wanted to."

"Exactly, but that's just the tip of the iceberg," Aaron said. "People don't realize how the government is tracking everything, although they should. It seems like every other week there's an article about another apology from Google for tracking this or that, and carrying an iPhone is like voluntarily letting someone track you. The social networking sites are essentially doing the same thing. Anyway, it would stun you to know how much information we have on people. My suggestion is to keep a low profile and simplify your life."

"Is that what you're doing?"

Aaron shook his head wistfully. ""I'm trying, but I think it's too late for me because of my job. I know too many secrets. I'm essentially caught in their web, so I'll have to ride out what's coming."

"Did they make you get the chip?" Nathan asked.

"Not yet, although they're really putting pressure on me. Thankfully it isn't a requirement yet for federal employees, but I'm sure that will be coming soon. So stay away from government jobs. I'd leave mine if I dared."

"Thanks for the advice, but I've actually been offered a job with the Church," Nathan said. "That's actually part of the reason why I'm here to talk with you."

"That's great! How can I help?"

Nathan shifted uncomfortably. "Well, you've probably noticed that Marie and I get along pretty well. I really like her, so I'm torn about the Church job. At first it seemed like it was heaven-sent. I'd be working in Salt Lake, and she'd be going to college there. But this internship in Chicago has thrown me for a loop. It feels completely wrong to me. From what I've heard, the protests and riots that happened across the country last year are expected to be even worse this summer, and it could be dangerous there."

Aaron nodded slowly. "I'm concerned about that as well, but let me ask you this. Is Marie the same girl you knew when you were in high school?"

"Well, she's as pretty and as fun as ever, but either I got a lot more spiritual, or . . ."

"I know what you're saying," Aaron said. "Carol and I have noticed it as well. We talk with her, and I really don't think she is breaking the Word of Wisdom or being immoral, but there's a worldliness that has crept into her soul. It really bothered us when we found out she hadn't been going to church."

"That shocked me, too," Nathan said. "She's basically the reason I even went to church at first, and now she's the inactive one!"

"At first we cracked down on her by expressing our disappointment and threatening to take away her car and so forth," Aaron said. "But we really didn't have much leverage and she called our bluff. After that, she wouldn't answer our calls or emails for two months. Finally we went to her apartment and apologized."

"How did she respond?" Nathan asked.

"She was happy to reconcile with us. She started coming home a couple of weekends a month, and she'd go to church with us. That's really kind of where we're at right now. I really think she feels she's doing fine, but we still worry about the influence her roommates have on her. Did you happen to meet them today?"

"I met Sheridan. She seems like a free spirit."

"That's an understatement. So to be honest, Carol and I are really hoping something works out between the two of you. I don't think you realize how obsessed Marie was about your bombing incident in Minnesota. She spent hours online reading all about it."

"Wow! I didn't know that."

Aaron smiled. "So I hate to tip Marie's hand, but she's pretty interested in you, which we're very happy about. You're a wonderful young man with a great future."

Nathan dipped his head, surprised at the kind words. "Thank you. That means a lot. But there are definitely some obstacles for us. I just don't feel good about the internship."

"Neither do we," Aaron said. "To us it could become a real nightmare."

"Did you tell her that?"

Aaron shook his head. "Because of our previous disputes, we acted happy about it when she told us about the offer. We hope it will fall through, but it doesn't sound like it will."

"Would it be all right if I talked to her about it?" Nathan asked.

"Yes. In fact, you're about the only one who might possibly change her mind."

Nathan shrugged. "All I can do is try. I'll plan on visiting her again on Friday after I learn more about my Church job. Thanks for talking with me. It really helped."

They stood up, and Aaron clasped Nathan's shoulder as they walked to the front door. "I'll tell Carol everything we talked about. She'll be pleased. Hopefully things will work out for all of us."

As Nathan drove home, the Spiral Dream once again crossed his mind. Marie's battle with her parents on the staircase now made sense, but as the dream had concluded they had still been standing on the second level. There was no indication of how it would end up. Would Marie eventually climb the stairs and join the Saints, or would she happily slide down the railing?

CHAPTER 10

That night Nathan could hardly concentrate during his shift at Toys-R-Us. There were too many options running through his mind. If he took the Church job, his personal life would be greatly affected, along with his contact with Marie.

About halfway through his shift, he had assured himself if he kept the Toys-R-Us job and convinced Marie to stay, then they could move forward with their relationship.

But as the hours went by, that option felt wrong. As he finished his shift, the Spirit told him what to do. He took off his badge and went to his shift manager.

"I'm sorry, but this is my last night."

The manager raised his eyebrows. "What? You can't just quit on me!"

"I'm afraid I can. I've got another job lined up," Nathan said as he punched his timecard a final time. "There are enough people looking for work that you shouldn't have any trouble finding my replacement."

Nathan went home and slept for a few hours, but he woke up feeling anxious. He worried that he'd been too hasty in his decision to quit his job, so he decided to spend Thursday afternoon in the Provo City Center Temple. He'd never been inside the remodeled structure, because it had been dedicated during his mission. He marveled at how the architects had created such a beautiful array of rooms inside the building's original shell.

After participating in an endowment session, Nathan prayed for several minutes in the Celestial Room until he received a strong confirmation from the Spirit that he should take the Church job, no matter how it affected his situation with Marie.

With that assurance, he traveled to Salt Lake on Friday morning. As he entered the Joseph Smith Memorial Building, he found himself walking along with several other clean-cut men his age dressed in suits.

"I think we're all going to the same place," one man commented. "We should have carpooled."

The others laughed, and Nathan felt comfortable being part of the group. They filed into the room where Nathan had met with Elder Miller. The room had been reorganized with three rows of chairs facing a screen. Nathan took a seat on the front row.

Within a minute Elder Miller of the Quorum of the Seventy entered the room. He stood before them with a broad smile.

"Welcome, brethren," Elder Miller said. "I'm pleased to see each of you here. I know it wasn't an easy decision. You're all recently returned missionaries in the prime of your lives, ready to move forward with college, careers, and marriage. Then you receive a vague job offer from the Church. You aren't given many details about it, but the Spirit has confirmed to you that you should be in this room on this date at this time. Is that correct?"

Elder Miller raised his hand to his own question, and all of the men in the room did likewise.

"I congratulate you," he said. "You've passed a key test of faith. There were other men invited to this meeting who aren't here, and that's a shame. Why is it a shame? Because the reality is that each of you were recommended for this job by a special witness of the Lord. How many of you were told about this opportunity by an apostle?"

Once again everyone's hands went up. Elder Miller continued, "That apostle was told by the Spirit to invite you to be part of this group. We call this the MM Project, short for the Maintenance Missionary Project. In a sense, you're about to embark on another mission, but rather than preaching the gospel, you'll be serving the Lord in a variety of other ways to help the Kingdom of God roll forward. If you aren't willing to devote all of your time, talents and resources to this effort, you may leave now."

Elder Miller waited quietly for several seconds, then to Nathan's surprise the man sitting next to him stood up. "I'm sorry," he muttered, and walked out of the room. Two other men followed behind him and shut the door.

Elder Miller got a grim look on his face. "We all must make difficult choices, don't we? But you'll be blessed for your willingness to serve the Lord. Now let's begin."

He picked up a remote control and hit a button. On the screen behind him appeared Doctrine & Covenants 45:26-32.

"The reason for your service is summed up in this scripture." Elder Miller said. "*And in that day shall be heard of wars and rumors of wars, and the whole earth shall be in commotion, and men's hearts shall fail them, and they shall say that Christ delayeth his coming until the end of the earth.*

"*And the love of men shall wax cold, and iniquity shall abound.*

"*And when the times of the Gentiles is come in, a light shall break forth among them that sit in darkness, and it shall be the fulness of my gospel;*

"*But they receive it not; for they perceive not the light, and they turn their hearts from me because of the precepts of men.*

"*And in that generation shall the times of the Gentiles be fulfilled.*

"*And there shall be men standing in that generation, that shall not pass until they shall see an overflowing scourge; for a desolating sickness shall cover the land.*

"*But my disciples shall stand in holy places, and shall not be moved; but among the wicked, men shall lift up their voices and curse God and die.*"

Elder Miller finished reading and faced the men. "The Prophet Joseph Smith received this revelation in 1831. Here we are more than 180 years later, on the verge of it being fulfilled. Ever since the Lord brought the Jaredites to the Americas, a promise has been made to the inhabitants of this chosen land. Do you know what that is?"

Nathan raised his hand and said, "If the people kept the commandments they would prosper in the land, but if they didn't, they would perish."

"That's right," Elder Miller said. "That promise is repeated over and over throughout the Book of Mormon and the Doctrine and Covenants. Our nation is still held to those same standards. How are Americans doing as a whole? In general, are we a God-fearing nation of righteous families that obeys Christian teachings?"

"No," several men said in unison.

"I agree. In many ways we have turned our backs to God. Our leaders and the laws they enact increasingly seem to be contrary to what the Bible teaches. I personally feel the Lord has been overly patient with our nation, but the time has come for a great change. As Latter-day Saints, though, we shouldn't despair. The Lord is watching out for us."

He faced the screen again and said, "Let me read one statement again: '*But my disciples shall stand in holy places, and shall not be moved.*' This is where each of you come in. Under the Lord's direction, through his prophets, the Church has quietly prepared places of refuge for the Saints to leave Babylon, if you will, and survive this coming sickness and destruction. Throughout the years the Church has acquired dozens of properties that are scattered throughout the mountains, away from civilization."

"The girls camps?" one man asked.

Elder Miller nodded. "Yes, some of these sites have been used as girls camps and already have nice facilities and plenty of provisions. But there are also many more areas where the Saints will gather that still need a stockpile of supplies and improved facilities."

A man raised his hand. "Are we the only men doing this? It seems like we could use a little more help."

Elder Miller chuckled. "Actually, those of you in this room are only a small part of a sizable group. There are more than 200 men already serving, and we expect to have more join us in the coming weeks. The planning for this exodus has been underway at high levels in the Church for years, and vast amounts of preparation have already gone into the effort. Senior missionary couples have devoted thousands of hours in preparing the camps, and now your main role will be to help them finish the job."

"When will the Church members go to these camps?" another man asked.

"It will come as an invitation from the First Presidency through the proper priesthood channels. I believe the plan for this area is for the bishops to receive a letter they'll be asked to read in Sacrament Meeting. At that point, the Saints must choose to accept the prophet's invitation or reject it. I assure you that no one will be forced to go against their will."

"How come we've never heard this?" the man asked. "Do the stake presidents and bishops even know what is planned?"

"A few do, and many wealthy Saints have already devoted much of their fortunes to buy land and supplies. But does your typical bishop know about it? No, because it currently isn't part of their stewardship. Their duties are to watch over their ward members. However, there will soon come a time when everyone will be made aware of the plan."

"Wow, that doesn't give families much time to prepare," the man responded.

Elder Miller raised his eyebrows. "Do you really feel the Saints haven't been warned over and over for the past fifty years? For decades the Church leaders have emphasized the need to be physically prepared with a year's supply of food, and more recently for at least a three-month supply."

"That's true," the man said.

"More importantly, the emphasis of many General Conference talks the past few years has been on spiritual preparation, particularly in being willing to follow the prophet. Many members have ignored the leaders' warnings, but thankfully a great number of Saints are going to gladly accept such an invitation."

Nathan raised his hand. "I agree completely. I know of many Church members who've had dreams and visions about these upcoming events. These people are wholeheartedly preparing for such an event, and they're eagerly looking forward to it. In fact, I've had such a dream myself."

The room went silent, then Elder Miller said, "Would you mind sharing it with us?"

"I'd be happy to."

"Come stand up here," Elder Miller said. "By the way, this is Nathan Foster. Some of you might recognize him as the missionary who saved Elder Smith's life in Minnesota not too long ago."

Nathan wished Elder Miller had left that part out, but it served a purpose, because as he looked across the room at the other men, he saw a new respect in their eyes.

Nathan took about five minutes giving them the details of his Spiral Dream and the three levels he saw. He also told about the people's varied responses to the prophet's words, but he didn't mention Marie specifically. The men were listening intently, and several of them nodded in agreement at several points.

As he finished, Elder Miller stood up and actually clapped a few times as he came to Nathan's side. "Thank you so much for sharing that with us, because your dream helps answer the biggest question we receive from some of the stake presidents and other leaders that know about our plans. Their question is 'Why go to all of this trouble? Is the purpose just to save ourselves from destruction?'"

Nathan shook his head. "There's a greater purpose than that. I feel the dream indicates the time has come for the Church members to become more refined as we prepare to build New Jerusalem. The Lord needs the most dedicated Saints to do that, and so this invitation to leave the world behind is a sifting process."

"Exactly," Elder Miller said. "I like the fact that in your dream the Church members are all on the so-called second level. When the prophet gives his invitation, it truly is going to cause a division in the Church. People will either accept the prophet's words and rise to the third level, or they'll reject the prophet and lose the Spirit in their lives, which will put them on the same plane as the rest of the world."

"That's right," Nathan said. "I know people who have a ton

of food storage and actually take pride in how much they've accumulated. That's great, but will they humble themselves enough to give the food to the Church and then go live in a camp? I don't know."

Elder Miller nodded and said, "That's why each family's spiritual preparation is so important. To be honest, we really don't expect a great percentage of families to go to the camps. Nearly all of the inactive members will basically laugh at us and say we're freaking out. After all, the president says the economy is doing great, right?"

Elder Miller rolled his eyes as the group chuckled. "Anyway, it's the ones who I call 'socially active' who will really struggle with it. These people might come to Church on Sunday but ignore the gospel the rest of the week. When it gets to be crunch time, will they actually follow the prophet? Or will they be like these three brethren who left us this morning at the last moment so they could continue their current lifestyles?"

Elder Miller patted Nathan on the back and motioned for him to return to his chair. "Thank you so much for sharing your dream with us. That's a perfect illustration of what this is all about."

Once Nathan was seated, Elder Miller said, "Before I let you go today, I want to cover a few more items. We'll meet in the lobby downstairs at 9 a.m. on Monday. From that moment on you'll be considered a Church missionary once again, and later that day we'll set you apart as one. Needless to say, keep yourselves clean and pure this weekend. Don't do something stupid."

The group laughed at his comment, but they knew it was crucial to keep their guard up.

"Should we bring our own car?" another man asked.

"No," Elder Miller said. "Please have someone drop you off or take public transportation. You won't need your own vehicle, so either sell it or give it away this weekend."

"Really?" the man asked in surprise. "Couldn't we just store it somewhere?"

"I suppose, but you'll likely never drive it again. We'll cover many more details on Monday, but for now please return to your homes and take care of any last-minute preparations. You really are leaving again on another mission. Close your cell phone account or give it away. As I mentioned, we'll provide everything you need, but you may bring one suitcase of clothes and other essential belongings."

"What do we tell our families we're doing?" Nathan asked.

"Simply explain that the Church has hired you for an extended period of time, and that the job will take you out of the area. Assure them that you'll be in touch when you can."

A man on the back row asked, "What's the timetable for when the prophet will write the letter? Has he given the General Authorities any indication about that?"

Elder Miller shrugged. "As you know, prophets almost never give specific dates in such matters, but the prophet has described the preparations for the mountain camps as 'urgent.' Let me describe it this way—the letter has already been written. Now it's just a matter of having the Lord tell the prophet when to have copies of the letter delivered to the bishops."

Those words sent a shock through the group. "It's close, then," one man said. "Like within a few months."

Elder Miller shook his head. "Not months. Weeks."

CHAPTER 11

When the meeting was over, Nathan felt a bit dazed by all of the information Elder Miller had shared with them. He was grateful he'd received such a strong confirmation in the temple about this decision, because he felt somewhat overwhelmed.

He knew he needed to talk to his father about what was happening in his life, but he also felt a great urgency to talk to Marie immediately. He called her, and he was relieved when she answered.

"Hi, Nathan," she said. "You know, you can always just text me if you want."

"I realize that, but I'm hoping we could get together this afternoon and talk. I'm in Salt Lake right now."

"That would be great!" Marie said. "So did you take the job with the Church?"

"Yeah. I just finished up getting more details about it. That's what I want to talk to you about."

"Is everything all right?" Marie asked.

"I'm fine, but I think you'd like to hear what they told me. Are you at your apartment?"

"I'm actually walking there right now."

"Could I pick you up in 15 minutes?"

"That will work," Marie said. "I'll watch for you."

Nathan soon pulled up in front of Marie's apartment. She

peeked out the window, waved, and then came out the door toward him wearing a red U of U shirt and jeans.

Nathan noticed she looked better than ever, which made what he had to say even more difficult. He was definitely smitten by her, but he knew he couldn't follow his heart.

He hopped out of the car as she approached and opened the passenger door for her.

"What a gentleman," she said, genuinely impressed. "I can't remember the last time a guy did that."

Once they were settled in the car, he pulled onto the road and asked, "How's everything going with your internship?"

Marie's eyes brightened. "Fantastic! I talked with Gretchen Howell and officially accepted it. They want me there a week from today so I can settle in and then start work the following Monday. I'm so excited!"

"It sounds like you'll have a great time there," Nathan said, trying to sound enthusiastic.

"I think so! They're an amazing company, and I know I'll learn a lot. I really want you to come visit me, though. You'd have to sleep on the couch, of course . . ."

"Of course," Nathan said. "Unfortunately, I don't know if I'll be able to make it out there because of this new job."

"Why not? Can't you take a few days off?"

"That's why I wanted to talk to you. This job is going to keep me tied up. They didn't even mention any vacation time."

Marie frowned. "Are you kidding me? They can't treat you like a slave."

"It's okay," Nathan said. "Actually, I'm a little worried about you going to Chicago. Aren't you?"

""Not really. You mean because of the unrest and rioting they've had there?"

"Yeah."

"I asked Gretchen about that, and she said it has all happened far from their headquarters. I'll be working in a skyscraper that's in a fancy part of town."

"That's good," Nathan said. "It's just that things there could get really bad fast. The country could unravel while you're there."

Marie stared at him, then started laughing. "Oh, I get it now. This is about us, right?"

Nathan shrugged, not quite sure how to respond. Marie put her hand on his shoulder and said, "I know we've been avoiding the obvious ever since you got home, but let me say that I'm really attracted to you. Is that too forward?"

"No. It's nice to hear," Nathan said. "I feel the same way about you."

Marie slid her hand down his arm and took his hand in hers. At this point, Nathan decided he'd better pull over to the curb. He stopped the car, and on impulse he leaned over and kissed her gently. She smiled at him and kissed him back.

Nathan was surprised at himself. He heard Elder Miller's voice in his head saying, "*Don't do something stupid.*"

He leaned back and asked, "How is this all going to work out? We like each other, but we seem to be going in different directions."

Marie frowned. "I understand how you feel. I don't want to be separated from you either, but this internship is the key to my future—our future! This will open up all kinds of doors for me after I graduate."

"That sounds wonderful," Nathan said hesitantly, "but have you prayed about it?"

Marie furrowed her brow, feeling a bit perturbed. "Of course I've prayed about it! That's the main reason I feel this internship is meant to be. I asked the Lord to help me get the internship, and I did! The odds were pretty slim that I'd get it, so I see the Lord's hand in it. I really don't think the Lord would have allowed me to get it if something bad was going to happen to me while I'm there."

Nathan was briefly speechless. Her reasoning almost made sense, but it didn't feel quite right. There was no use arguing, though. He knew her mind was made up.

"I can't really dispute that," he said. "Go to Chicago and have a great experience."

"Thank you," she said, giving him another kiss.

Nathan knew he had to add one more detail. "I hate to say this, but I start working for the Church on Monday. I think they're going to throw us right into some big project without any time off, so I'm hoping you'll be coming to Orem on Sunday so we can say good-bye."

"I'll be there," she said. "I need to get some things packed at my parents' house anyway."

Marie had to get to an afternoon class, so Nathan dropped her off at her apartment. They kissed good-bye, then she got out of the car and said, "See you Sunday!"

She shut the door and Nathan watched her walk away. She was everything he had ever dreamed of.

He drove through Salt Lake with a huge smile on his face, but as he reached I-15, reality began to set in. Yes, if the world didn't change for a few years, then they might actually end up together, although just that morning he'd heard a General Authority say the conditions in the United States were about to be drastically altered.

He shook his head in disappointment at himself. He'd arranged to meet with Marie so he could convince her to drop her internship. Instead, they had ended up kissing a few times and her internship plans were more solid than ever.

His head was swirling. Maybe his Church job would only last a few months, then it would all work out. He truly hoped so.

CHAPTER 12

As Nathan drove back to Orem that afternoon, he was fretting so much about his relationship with Marie that he hadn't even turned on the car radio, so he didn't hear the news reports until he got home. When he walked in the door, Vanessa called to him from the front room. "Have you heard what happened?" she asked. "Southern California got hit by a huge earthquake today."

He joined her and Denise in front of the TV and watched as a skyscraper became engulfed in flames. The report soon switched to footage from a helicopter that clearly showed where a fault line had opened up, creating a deep gash across the landscape. Homes were tumbling into the void, and roads disappeared into it.

"How big was the quake?" Nathan asked.

"They're saying it was a 7.6," Vanessa said. "There have been several strong aftershocks already. I'm so worried. I have a sister and brother who live down there. I've tried calling them, but the lines are all jammed."

They continued to watch as reports came in from several different locations. Since it hit in the early afternoon, millions of people were trapped away from their homes. Several key freeways were cracked and unusable, and fires seemed to be sprouting up everywhere. They showed another shot where an entire block of homes had been jolted and now all sharply tilted in one direction.

"This is terrible," Nathan said. "The damages are going to be in the billions of dollars."

Garrett soon arrived home, and they all watched until the news reports started repeating themselves. Vanessa began preparing dinner, and Nathan said to Garrett, "Can we talk for a minute?"

They went into the living room, and Garrett asked, "What's going on?"

"I've got a new job offer, and I think I'm going to take it."

"Really?" Garrett asked. "Who with?"

"The Church. When I was on my mission Elder Smith of the Quorum of the Twelve told me about this opportunity, and so I followed up on it last week. They want me to start on Monday."

"Wow, that's fast," Garrett said. "What will you be doing?"

"It's mainly humanitarian work, such as delivering supplies and building shelters. I'll have housing in Salt Lake, but it sounds like I'll be traveling a lot."

"Well, if you're happy with it, then I support you. Besides, I sensed the Toys-R-Us job wasn't going to last forever."

"Thanks, Dad. The hardest part will be not living here. I've really started to bond with Vanessa and Denise—and you."

"I feel the same way. But you'll be able to visit, right?"

"Once in a while," Nathan said. "They said they'll provide all of the transportation I need, so I won't be using my car. Since you made the down payment, I'll let you decide what to do with it."

Garrett raised his eyebrows. "Won't you need it when the job is done?"

"Maybe, but they said this job could last several months."

Hmm. I guess I'll just park it in the driveway with a 'For Sale' sign and see if there are any takers."

"Thanks, Dad. Please don't think I'm not appreciative of everything you've done for me since I got home. It has really meant a lot to me."

"No problem," Garrett said. "It's the least I could do."

❧

During dinner, they talked some more about the earthquake, which led Nathan to tell Vanessa and Denise about his new job and that he'd be moving out. They weren't very happy about it, but they said they supported his decision. After dinner, Nathan felt prompted to take Denise out for a treat. He stopped by her bedroom where she was listening to music.

"Hey, would it be all right if I treated you to some dessert?"

Denise seemed surprised, but said, "Sure!"

They let Vanessa and Garrett know where they were going, then they got in the car and started driving.

"What would you like?" he asked.

"Let's split a dozen Krispy Kreme donuts," she said with a smile. "Mom never lets me eat those."

"Sounds good to me!"

Within a few minutes they had each picked out six donuts and a drink. They moved to a table in the store. Denise quickly sat down and selected a creme-filled one. She bit halfway through it and got it all over her face.

"Oh, that's so good," she mumbled.

Nathan laughed, admiring this younger sister he barely knew. Once they had both eaten three donuts, they took a break.

"Denise, I want you to know you can always count on me. No matter what happens, I'm your brother. Don't ever forget that."

She smiled. "It's nice to a have a big brother. I'm sad you're moving to Salt Lake, though. You'll have to visit as often as you can, okay?"

"I'll certainly try." Nathan looked at the remaining six donuts. "I think I'm full. How about you?"

"I'm getting there."

"We could take the rest of these home to our parents . . ."

Denise looked betrayed. "I've got a better idea. How about if my big brother smuggles them up to my bedroom?"

Nathan smiled. "You've got a deal."

CHAPTER 13

Halfway across the world, a diplomat named Chen Ming walked through a bustling crowd in Beijing, China. He had been summoned for an urgent meeting with his superiors.

It was a nice morning, and seemingly everyone wanted to be outside. He was accustomed to the city's endless commotion—after all, he'd grown up there—but as he settled into middle age he was eager for the upcoming changes he knew were coming in his life.

He had enjoyed a nice supper the previous evening with his parents to celebrate their 55th wedding anniversary, but now he was focused on his upcoming assignment.

He reached the conference room and saw several key people gathered around a TV screen. He saw one of his close friends and asked, "Why did we need to meet today? What has happened?"

"Hi, Dragon," his friend said. "There was a big earthquake in the United States. This might be the opportunity we've been waiting for."

Dragon smiled at his friend's use of the nickname he'd gained during their time together at the Chinese Embassy in Washington D.C. He'd received the name when one of his supervisors there found out his birth in 1964 had fallen in the Chinese calendar's Year of the Dragon.

"Nobody's called me Dragon since I left the United States," he said. "I've missed it."

The friend smiled. "We might as well use it again, since you're heading back there."

Soon Dragon was seated around a table with other Chinese

leaders, and they all agreed to speed up their plans after the earthquake.

"This disaster is going to have far-reaching effects across the United States," one diplomat said. "Their economy is going to take a hit, and if we implement our plan as quickly as possible, it will be a powerful one-two punch."

Dragon smiled. The timing was right, and America would never suspect the source of their troubles. China had purposely acted like a big lovable panda bear in their dealings with the United States for the past two decades, and it had paid off both diplomatically and economically. However, the Americans didn't seem to realize that when a panda is irritated, it will occasionally violently attack—and China was definitely irritated with America.

The meeting soon concluded, and Dragon departed to begin his assignment as quickly as possible. He returned to the modern office tower where he lived, exchanging pleasantries with the doorman before stepping into the nearby elevator and being whisked to his penthouse suite on the tenth floor.

He entered his suite, gently shut the door, and then stood motionless for nearly a minute, savoring the silence. He moved to a large window that overlooked the sprawling city. The unrelenting haze of pollution obscured the rising sun, and he shook his head at the unending mass of humanity on the streets below.

"I can't wait to get out of here," he said quietly. He had already selected his future home once this assignment was over—a large ranch house in America tucked away in a quiet valley where he could actually see the stars at night.

Dragon moved from the window and pondered the direction his life had taken. As a young man he had excelled in his studies and had been given the chance to attend college in the United States. After graduating with a bachelor's degree from the University of Maryland in the early 1990s, he returned to China and worked his way through the political ranks.

He was eventually assigned to work in the Chinese Embassy in Washington, D.C., where he was trusted and well-liked. His superiors had recognized his skills and groomed him for more important projects. After numerous successes in the service of the Chinese government, he was on the verge of his crowning achievement before retirement. This upcoming mission would make him revered among his countrymen forever.

❧

By mid-morning Dragon was ready to depart on his journey. He wandered through his apartment for the last time, retrieving a few remaining personal items. All of the furnishings in the apartment were staying there, since another Chinese leader would take up residency in the penthouse in a few days.

After his belongings were packed, he went to a small closet and removed a sturdy briefcase that had been delivered to him the previous week. He carried it to the kitchen table, entered the correct numbers in the combination lock, then carefully opened it. Inside were four metallic thermos-type containers. Each one was about the size of a soda can and bound tightly in bubble wrap to avoid any mishaps. He gingerly touched each one.

"Everything looks good," he said before snapping the briefcase shut. He placed it back in the closet and then smiled in wonderment at what those four small packages would soon help trigger—the downfall of the United States.

CHAPTER 14

On Sunday, Nathan had expected to see Marie at church, but her parents said she wouldn't be coming to Orem until that evening. It made him uneasy. He was sure she would've wanted to spend the day with him.

He texted her after the meetings, and she responded that she'd be at her parents' home by 5 p.m. and that she had some items to discuss. He immediately called her, but she didn't answer. Something strange was definitely going on.

Nathan spent the afternoon with his family as more reports came in about the California earthquake. Vanessa had been able to reach her siblings, and although their homes had been damaged, they and their families had escaped serious injuries.

However, more than 1,000 deaths had been reported, and even the most optimistic estimates indicated that everyday life wouldn't return to normal there for several weeks. The destruction of the freeway system had paralyzed the whole region.

As Nathan watched the scenes of destruction, he felt strongly that he should convince Marie to stay in Utah. This earthquake was going to have a ripple effect on the nation's economy, and could lead to more unrest, especially in Chicago.

At five o'clock he drove over to the Shaws' home, and it was obvious he was interrupting a family fight as Aaron opened the door. Marie had tears in her eyes, and her parents looked angry.

Nathan stepped cautiously into the front room. "Should I come back later?"

"No, we need to talk things out," Aaron said.

Marie came to him and took hold of his arm. "They're trying to get me to cancel my internship. That's why I stayed in Salt Lake until this afternoon."

Carol shook her head. "We're just worried you haven't thought things through. I saw on the news that two more companies are moving their headquarters out of Chicago because of all the violence there lately."

"I'll be fine!" Marie screamed at her. "What are you so scared about? I told you I'll be in the safest part of the city."

Aaron tried to stay calm as he said, "Look at all the looting and murders that are already happening so fast in California. You know the Carters? They went on vacation there last week, but the bishop said they're stuck now and are in real danger. It just seems like the whole nation is on edge, and things could explode. I don't want to send you out into it."

Everyone stood tensely for a moment before Nathan said quietly, "Your parents are right."

"Now you're on their side?" Marie asked incredulously. "Was everything you told me on Friday a big lie?"

"No, but you don't seem to realize it's dangerous out there, and it's going to get worse! You're a beautiful woman going alone to a city filled with thugs. What good is an internship if you wind up dead?"

Marie wiped away some tears. "You sound just like my dad. All my life I've heard nothing but doomsday predictions. 'Joseph Smith said this, John Taylor said that.' He's been talking about the last days for as long as I can remember, and what has happened? Nothing! Absolutely nothing!"

"That's not true," Nathan said. "The prophecies are all coming together, and it's going to be a huge mess. You need to stay close to home."

Marie gave him an exasperated look. "Some of those prophecies are nearly 200 years old, and it could be another century before they come true. I highly doubt the world is going to collapse during my four months in Chicago."

She backed away from him like a caged animal. "Don't you realize how hard I worked to get this internship? I beat out more than a thousand applicants! I'm going, no matter what any of you say."

She marched across the room to the stairway then turned around. "Nathan, I think you better leave. I care about you, but if you can't support me on this, then things just aren't going to work out between us. Don't call me again."

She then climbed the stairs without looking back. Carol started crying and excused herself, and Aaron looked devastated.

Nathan felt sick inside and turned toward the door, but Aaron grabbed his arm and whispered, "Hey, you said the right things. I admire you for that."

Nathan sighed. "I suppose, but it feels like my heart has been stomped on."

"I understand, but don't give up on her. You're the best thing that has happened to her in a long time."

Nathan shrugged. "I'll check in with you in a few days after she's gone, but I think for now I'll do as she said and leave her alone."

"That's probably best," Aaron said. "She can be stubborn, so just give her some space."

"I will. You know what? I really hope she's right about the future, and that we're wrong."

"Believe me, Nathan. So do I."

CHAPTER 15

Nathan's emotions were still running high the next morning when he arrived at the Joseph Smith Building. He hadn't slept very well after his confrontation with Marie, but he knew he'd made the right decision. If he was meant to be with her, it wasn't going to happen anytime soon.

Garrett had given him a ride to Salt Lake, and he was one of the first to arrive, but soon several other men that he recognized entered the lobby. Everyone seemed to be in good spirits.

Suddenly Elder Miller was in the midst of them. "A bus will be arriving outside within five minutes," he said. "Before you board the bus, use the tags we've provided to label your suitcases and backpacks. Your belongings will be waiting for you at our destination. As you board the bus, make sure the attendant checks off your name."

Once the bus was loaded, the men hardly spoke as they traveled to the Bishop's Central Storehouse located at 5400 West near I-80 in Salt Lake. The bus passed through a parking lot and stopped at a side entrance, where the men were ushered into the building. They walked down a hall and came to a spacious well-lit room that had several charts and maps on the walls.

Elder Miller had somehow arrived before them, and he waited patiently as they gathered in a semi-circle around him.

"Congratulations once again on accepting this assignment," he said. "Today we'll test your aptitude in a variety of assignments. From this group we'll assign scouts, guards, nurses, cooks, messengers, animal herders, and delivery personnel. But first we want to give

71

you an overview of what we expect from you. Just follow me as we move around the room and stop at several stations."

At the first station the men gathered around a table that held a key, a cell phone, and a handgun.

"After you've been given a specific assignment, you'll be placed in an apartment with a missionary who has the same task. We've recently built a series of apartments within walking distance of this building, and that's where you'll stay when you are in Salt Lake. Some of your assignments might take you out of the area for a few days at a time, and accommodations have been made for you in those cases. As I mentioned in our first meeting, several other groups of maintenance missionaries are already working, so we've worked out most of the kinks in the system."

He picked up the three items. "You'll be given a key to your apartment, and it will have your room number stamped on it. Your cell phone will be programmed with certain numbers that pertain to your assignment. You aren't permitted to call or receive calls from anyone else."

Elder Miller then held up the handgun and asked, "Have you all shot one of these before?"

Everyone raised their hands, although Nathan did hesitantly, because he hadn't shot one since his days as a Boy Scout. He was quite sure he wasn't going to be a guard.

"It looks unanimous," Elder Miller said as he scanned the raised hands. "Your gun will help protect you in times of danger, although we hope you'll never have to use it. You'll all receive one, unless you're a complete failure during the testing and we decide you're a danger to yourself."

The group laughed, and Elder Miller moved a few feet forward to a large glass window that looked out over the immense warehouse.

"This building is nearly 600,000 square feet and the entire property covers more than 35 acres," he said. "We have the capacity to store 65,000 pallets of food and supplies here, and as it is hauled away, we replace it with products from the many canneries and meat packing plants we have throughout the region. It's an amazing process. Never doubt whether the Lord will provide for his Saints."

The group moved down the wall and soon stood in front of a huge map of the United States that was covered by dozens of white and blue circular stickers. Each sticker had a number in the center. Elder Miller motioned toward the map.

"Each dot represents a Church camp site. Did you realize the Church owned this many camps? As you can see, there are more than 200 sites that have been designated as places where the Saints can gather. The white dots are what we consider the best camps and most of them are in the Rocky Mountains. They're the farthest from civilization and are basically undetectable unless you're right at the entrance. They've been modernized in many ways and are actually quite nice."

"Who gets to live there?" a missionary asked.

"These camps are for the Saints who respond to the prophet's invitation," Elder Miller said. "They'll be organized under the direction of the priesthood and have the strongest defenses. As you can see, about half of the camps fall into that category."

He then motioned toward the eastern United States. "We've created several of these 'best camps' throughout the country. Some of them are quite close to a temple, and we already have fencing materials in place so they'll be able to create a secure compound that encloses both the temple and the camp sites."

"I'm impressed at how everything is already in motion," one man said. "What are the Saints doing in other countries?"

"They're going to gather to their closest temple or stake center, and the Area Presidencies across the world are working out the details for each stake," Elder Miller said. "Over the past several years the Church has sent thousands of shipments across the world to help these Saints have a stockpile of items, and at this point they'll be fine. In actuality those Saints are quite self-sufficient and will endure the coming economic problems very well. It's the Saints here in the United States that we're the most worried about."

He pointed at the map again. "As you can see, there are also blue dots that represent other camps. Our hope is that when the prophet's letter is sent out there's an overwhelming positive response from the Saints, but we're realistic that the initial response will be fairly small. However, as national conditions get steadily worse in the weeks that follow, some members will realize they should've followed the prophet. They'll try to find out where the first groups of Saints went, but they won't be able to locate them.

"So we're preparing for this so-called 'second wave' of Saints by creating the blue camps. The members will have to get there on their own, and there will be minimal Church organization there, although we'll provide guards. We'll stock these camps fairly well with food as time permits, but the accommodations won't be too great. We aren't trying to punish these people or anything, but they'll have had their chance to respond to the prophet's invitation just like everyone else."

"Will they ever have an opportunity to join the other Saints?" another missionary asked.

"Possibly, but not for a while," Elder Miller said. "We hope that some of these members will be spiritually strengthened there and eventually rejoin the rest of the Saints when we assemble in larger groups. Any other questions?"

A man raised his hand. "My neighbor has a nice cabin deep in the Uinta Mountains stocked with a two-year supply of food. He says if there's any major trouble, he's taking his family there to hide out and defend themselves against intruders. What do you think about that?"

"Is this man active in the Church?"

"Yes. He's on our stake high council."

"Hmm," Elder Miller said. "We've actually discussed these situations, because there are a lot of members who are already prepared and could live for months on their own. The trouble is that even though it would probably be easier for him and his family to live on their own, the Lord needs leaders like him in these camps."

The man nodded. "I doubt he knows about the Church's plans, so maybe he'll switch gears and join the Saints when he hears about the prophet's invitation."

"I hope so. In those situations we would help him retrieve his food storage and take it to his Church camp, because the Lord really needs his strongest and most experienced Saints there to help the camps run smoothly. That's why the prophet's letter will invite all Saints to gather to the camps—the rich and the poor. After all, this gathering has a greater purpose than just physically surviving the coming troubles. As we said in one of our meetings, it will also help the Saints become spiritually refined and achieve a higher level of unity—a Zion community, if you will. After all, it is these Saints who will soon build New Jerusalem."

One missionary raised his hand. "So are you saying that after the Saints have been in these camps, they won't return to their homes?"

"That's correct. We have much to do to prepare for the Second Coming of Christ, and a crucial step, to quote the Tenth Article of Faith, is 'that Zion (the New Jerusalem) will be built upon the American continent.' That is our ultimate purpose."

CHAPTER 16

After a few more minutes of instruction by Elder Miller, the missionaries were given a light lunch. During the lunch break, they were individually taken into a room with Elder Miller and another leader and formally set apart to serve as a full-time missionary for the Church.

Nathan listened carefully to his blessing and felt a surge of power pass through him as Elder Miller promised that angels would be watching over him to protect and guide him. He was also promised that opportunities would come to give healing priesthood blessings, and he would witness many miracles in the coming months.

After the blessing, Nathan turned around to shake hands with the men and thank them for their inspired words. Elder Miller smiled at him and said, "The Lord has great things in store for you, Nathan."

After eating, they were asked to fill out a questionnaire that gauged their interests and skills. As Nathan went through it, he realized he had no desire to herd animals or work as a medical assistant. Besides, he didn't have any experience in either of those areas. He'd been required to get a Commercial Drivers License to work at Toys-R-Us, though, so he made special mention of that on his questionnaire.

The group soon moved outside, where the men were put through their series of tests, including shooting a handgun and driving a large moving van through a maze of orange cones. Nathan did okay on the shooting test, but he really excelled at the driving exam. He had the fastest time and didn't hit a cone.

By late afternoon, the men were divided into six different groups. Nathan found himself standing in the parking lot next to seven other men. A middle-aged man walked over to them.

"Hello, I'm Samuel Pickering, and I'm the coordinator for our fleet of delivery vans. The eight of you have been selected to serve in one of our most important assignments—getting the food supplies from this warehouse to the camps. You'll each be assigned your own truck, and each day you'll have a delivery to complete. You saw the map inside of all the various camps. Some are within a day's drive, while others will take longer."

He motioned toward a set of housing units in the distance. "In a few minutes I'll take you over to your living quarters. They're actually one-bedroom apartments that were originally used by senior missionary couples who worked in the storehouse, but our circumstances have obviously changed."

A missionary asked, "Do we have an assigned companion?"

Samuel shook his head. "One difference in this round of your missionary service is that although you have a roommate, you don't have a designated companion. Sometimes you'll work with others, but often you'll be working on your own, particularly as we transport items to the camps. Time is short, and we need every one of you. You'll be staying busy now that the snow on the mountain roads is melting and we can get the supplies to the camps."

"Aren't the camps well-stocked already?" one man asked.

"No, most of these sites were used as girls camps or Boy Scout camps well into last autumn, so there wasn't space available to store the supplies," Samuel said. "Can you imagine leaving a pile of food within reach of hungry Scouts? That's not a good idea!"

The group chuckled, then Samuel added, "Besides, I've heard through the grapevine that the prophet didn't have a distinct impression on the timing of the coming national problems until a few weeks ago, so that's why we're hurrying now."

"What clothes will we wear?" Nathan asked. "Do we have a uniform?"

"No, you'll wear regular work clothes—a nice shirt, jeans, and comfortable boots that we'll provide for you. Your main objective is to blend in. The General Authorities will never say it, but I will—let your hair grow. Even look a little scruffy. We want you to essentially be hidden from the world, even though you'll be among them every day. No one will realize what you're doing."

Some of the men smiled at each other. "This is going to be a lot of fun," one said.

Samuel turned on him. "This isn't a laughing matter. There are people out there who want to kill you! Unless you find ways to evade them and escape their plots against us, they'll get you."

Samuel's comment silenced the group. He finally said, "Sorry I spoke that way, but one of our drivers was shot last week and is still in the hospital. He thinks he was targeted, so please take this seriously. Well, let's show you your new homes."

They walked to the apartment complex and found their suitcases waiting for them. Then Samuel gave them each a key and let them go inspect their new living quarters. Nathan's key was stamped with a "7" and as he approached the door, he saw a muscular, blond man standing in the doorway.

"Welcome," the man said. "I'm Chet, your roommate. Come on in."

Nathan entered the apartment and could smell a delicious aroma coming from the small kitchen.

"I'm guessing this isn't your first day," Nathan said.

"No I've been serving for two weeks," Chet said. "It'll be great to finally have a roommate. Where are you from?"

"Orem. I got home from my mission to Minnesota just a few weeks ago. How about you?"

"I'm from Fillmore and got home from Oklahoma about two months ago."

Nathan noticed some well-worn work gloves on a chair. "So I suppose you're already making deliveries?"

"Yep. I just got back from delivering cans of wheat to a camp near Logan. It wasn't too bad."

The two men hit it off quickly, and as Chet pulled a loaf of bread from the oven, there was a knock on the door. Nathan opened it and saw Samuel standing there. He came in and put two manila envelopes on the table, then handed Nathan a bag that held a cell phone, a handgun and two boxes of bullets.

"Nathan, these envelopes hold your assignments for the week. Chet, go over the basics with Nathan tonight, and let me know if you have any concerns. I'm not worried, though. You did well today on your driving."

"Thank you," Nathan said. "I'll do my best."

"Also, my cell number is the first one listed in your phone. Call me if you have any questions or problems during a delivery."

Meanwhile. Chet had buttered three pieces of bread and now handed one to Nathan and Samuel before taking a bite out of his own piece. They all savored the taste, then Samuel said, "You lucked out with your roommate, Nathan. Everyone here is top-notch, but no one can cook like Chet."

࿐

After Samuel left, the pair spent several minutes going over their upcoming assignments. Nathan saw he would be making daily deliveries to a camp near Vernal, Utah.

"Do they usually send you to the same place every day?" he asked.

"Yeah, at least for the first week," Chet said. "It lets you get the hang of things. Then they'll start sending you on longer trips. It looks like I'll be heading into Canada, so I might not make it back for a few of days. It looks like you'll be cooking for yourself a few times this week!"

"Where do I sleep if I don't make it back in one day?" Nathan asked.

"The guys who do the schedules try to make it work for you to be able to stay at a Church camp, but sometimes I've slept in my truck at rest stops along the way. You do what you have to do."

"Do we load everything in by hand?" Nathan asked.

"No, thank goodness," Chet said. "Sometimes you do when you unload at a camp, but here they use a forklift to load the truck each night. The trucks are ready to go first thing in the morning. We'll be down at the loading dock at 7 a.m."

"Then I'm on my own?"

"Yep," Chet said with a grin. "They throw you right into it, but I can tell you'll do great."

CHAPTER 17

As Nathan spent a busy week taking loads of supplies each day to the camp near Vernal, Marie packed her bags for Chicago. She surprised her parents on Thursday night by returning home and patching up their differences. She apologized for her bad attitude and promised to call them every day.

Carol took her to Salt Lake International Airport on Friday morning, and as the plane took off, Marie realized she wouldn't see Nathan for a few months. She hated to admit it, but she was annoyed that Nathan had taken her seriously and hadn't called her. The previous night she had given in and called his cell phone, but all she got was a computerized voice saying his number was no longer in service.

"All I can do is look forward to this new adventure," she told herself. "The Church job will keep Nathan busy, and he'll still be there at the end of the summer. Maybe this is for the best."

By mid-afternoon, she was looking out the plane window at the flat expanses of rural Illinois. The patchwork of fields seemed to go on forever without a mountain in sight. Soon the plane's captain asked them to fasten their seatbelts, and as the plane descended Marie stared out at the green suburbs of Chicago. Everything looked lush and tranquil.

"This is what all the fuss was about?" she muttered. "Nathan made it sound like they were rioting in the streets."

The plane touched down at Chicago's O'Hare International Airport, and as she exited the plane and entered the concourse, she saw a thin woman with long blonde hair holding a sign with her name on it. Marie walked over and said, "Hello! I'm Marie."

The woman's face brightened. "Welcome! I'm Bianca Ashman. Gretchen Howell sent me in her behalf. She wanted to see you before the end of the day, so I'll take you directly to her office after we retrieve your luggage."

"Thank you," Marie said. "I'm so excited to be here."

"You're going to have a wonderful time," Bianca said. "Just like you, I started out with Naples & Austin as a summer intern, and now I'm Gretchen's personal assistant. So the sky's the limit!"

◆

After picking up Marie's two suitcases, the women made their way to the main parking garage, where they slipped the luggage into the back of a silver Honda CR-Z.

"It was either this or my Ferrari," Bianca said with a smile. "But I wasn't sure how much luggage you'd have!"

Marie sensed Bianca wasn't joking. "It sounds like this is a great company to work for," Marie said.

"It's the best," Bianca said as she drove the car onto I-90 heading east. "You'll love it."

"The city looks peaceful," Marie said. "My parents and boyfriend acted like I was moving to a war zone."

Bianca shrugged. "The Bloomingdale's Building where we work is about as risk-free as you can get, but Chicago does have some dangerous places. Just use common sense. I grew up about 100 miles south of here, and I've seen a few things, but if you follow some basic rules of thumb, you should be fine."

"Like what?" Marie asked.

"You know, stick to well-lit places with lots of other people around, don't jog in the park after dark—and don't consume lots of alcohol before you stumble home alone."

Marie laughed. "Is that from personal experience?"

"No comment, but my martial arts training sure came in handy that night!"

Just then an 18-wheeler swerved in front of them. Bianca let out a string of profanities, taking Marie by surprise.

Once Bianca had calmed down a bit, Marie said, "Yeah, that guy was an idiot. Anyway, tell me about the Bloomingdale's Building. I read that it's 66-stories high."

"The building has everything you'd ever need," Bianca said. "I have a condo there, and some days I don't even go outside. It has a huge atrium that I like to go sit in when I need some time to myself, and the mall is great."

"It sounds amazing," Marie said.

They were silent for a moment before Bianca cocked her head and looked over at Marie. "By the way, did I hear you say 'boyfriend' a few moments ago?"

Marie shrugged. "Yeah, I guess you'd say that, but we're on a break for the summer."

"Good. I don't want anything to stop you from hanging out with us on the weekends."

"Okay, but I don't drink."

"Yeah, Gretchen had said you were a Mormon, so I figured as much. But don't worry, you'll still have fun, and you can help me get home!"

Just then Marie caught sight of the Magnificent Mile, an imposing row of skyscrapers where their building was located.

"This view is still impressive every time," Bianca said.

❧

Thirty minutes later, the women were walking into the main lobby of Naples & Austin, each carrying one of Marie's suitcases. Bianca stopped at the front desk and introduced Marie to the receptionist Alexis.

"It's a pleasure to meet you," Alexis said with a big smile. "Gretchen told me earlier we should get you processed before you meet with her. Please just run your chip over this scanner and you'll be set!"

Marie was momentarily speechless. Finally she said, "Uh, I haven't got the chip yet."

Bianca and Alexis looked at each other in surprise. Bianca finally said, "That's okay. There's a chip implantation center down in the mall. We'll take care of it after you talk with Gretchen."

Soon Marie was walking into Gretchen's office, and her new boss came around the desk and gave her a quick embrace. "It's wonderful you could come before the semester was over."

"Everything worked out well," Marie said. "My professors were very understanding."

"I'm grateful for that," Gretchen said. "And I suppose you got to know Bianca during your ride from the airport?"

"Yes, we hit it off right from the start," Marie said.

"Excellent," Gretchen said. "Bianca is a fantastic help to me. She enjoys the nightclub scene, but she's always here on Monday morning bright and early, raring to go to work."

"Yes, she seems to be top-notch."

Gretchen then glanced at her door to make sure it was closed before saying, "I hope you don't emulate her. I had thousands of women to choose for this internship, and I chose you. Do you know why?"

"Actually, no."

"You're immensely talented, which truly helped, but during our interview you told me about your high moral standards, which I've found to be severely lacking among the internship candidates in recent years. So if Bianca or Alexis invite you out on the town, I hope you follow that Wisdom Word you were telling me about. I'd actually be quite disappointed if you don't."

"Don't worry," Marie said. "During our drive here Bianca invited me to go out with her this weekend, and I explained that I don't drink."

"How did she respond?"

Marie smiled, "She was fine with it, partly because she's knows I'll still be sober at the end of the night!"

They then discussed several responsibilities Marie would

handle during the internship, and Gretchen explained that to enter a restricted part of the building she'd have to run her chip across a scanner on the door.

Marie raised her right hand. "Um, that might be a problem. As I told Alexis as I came in, I haven't received the chip yet."

Gretchen looked perplexed. "Really? Is it against your religion to get the chip?"

Marie shrugged. "It's discouraged, but not forbidden."

"Would you be willing to get it?" Gretchen asked. "Honestly, without the chip you won't function very well in many of the assignments I have planned for you."

Marie's heart was beating rapidly, but after a moment's hesitation, she nodded. "Yes, that would be fine. Bianca mentioned she could take me to an implantation center this evening."

Gretchen smiled widely. "Fantastic! You'll love it and wonder why you never got it before."

৵

The following morning Aaron Shaw arrived early at the NSA Data Center. He had expected Naples & Austin to give Marie an ultimatum about getting the chip, and he hoped she'd have the courage to tell them she couldn't—thus disqualifying her from the internship.

However, she had sounded thrilled with how everything was going when they'd talked to her the night before. She described her new apartment and told them about the new friends she'd already made—but she didn't mention anything about getting the chip.

The urge to know if Marie had gotten the chip had nagged at him all night, and he finally decided to go into work and find out, even though it was a Saturday.

The NSA offices were a flurry of activity seven days a week, so his presence didn't seem unusual to anyone. He waved to some co-workers as he reached his desk, then he logged onto his computer and entered Marie's basic information into the national database.

Within seconds a screen popped up listing Marie's vital statistics, as well as a recent photo of her. Next to the photo was a box that read "Chip implanted" and gave the implantation date as the previous evening.

He quickly typed in a password that allowed him to monitor her location through the GPS device embedded in her chip. Her present location was in her apartment inside the Bloomingdale's Building. He hit another key to trace her movements in the hours since the chip was implanted. He scrolled down and saw that she'd been at a nightclub until nearly 2 a.m.

"Wow, she's been gone less than two days and is already out on the town," he muttered.

His head began to pound as he resisted the urge to call her right then, but he knew it wasn't wise. He hated to spy on his daughter's activities, but he needed to keep this tracking ability as the ace up his sleeve.

Aaron switched to another screen that he had bookmarked—the profile of a man known as "Brix" on the streets of Chicago. The NSA had identified this convicted felon as the leader of a growing underground offshoot of the Occupy movement. Brix's group also wanted to bring down the supposed "one percent" but was planning a more sinister way to do so—murdering them in public areas. The FBI was keeping track of Brix and his followers, watching for any chance to arrest him, but so far Brix was a free man.

Aaron typed in the GPS password to see where Brix was that morning. His skin crawled as he saw Brix's location—inside a vehicle driving down the Magnificent Mile.

"That's just too close for comfort," Aaron whispered, feeling completely helpless concerning his daughter. "Heavenly Father, please watch over my sweet Marie."

CHAPTER 18

That spring the national debate over same-sex marriage had heated up again, and surveys indicated that the majority of Americans favored it being legalized nationwide. As the support grew, the Church faced extreme pressure from all sides to change its stance against it. Groups of protesters standing outside Church buildings were now common across the country, with the media seemingly always there to report any incidents. The tension escalated, though, when members of the First Presidency received a series of death threats and the walls of Temple Square were painted with obscene graffiti.

After consulting with Salt Lake City's public safety officials, the First Presidency announced that General Conference would still go forward as usual during the first weekend in April. However, the security precautions around Temple Square would be unprecedented.

In order to help prepare for General Conference, Nathan's assignment was temporarily switched from making deliveries to helping with security. He and dozens of other maintenance missionaries dressed in suits and stationed themselves around the Conference Center looking for any suspicious behavior.

The Church didn't limit anyone's freedom of speech, but the maintenance missionaries would stand directly in front of protestors and just stare into their eyes. The protesters seemed baffled at how to respond, and many simply stopped talking and walked away.

"Aw, come on," a middle-aged woman shouted at Nathan. "You guys aren't giving us a fair chance to voice our opinion."

Nathan just stared at her with his arms crossed as she continued to rant for another five minutes. She finally got right in his face, and he gently said, "If you touch me, you'll go straight to jail."

His response startled her, causing her to back away as if he had leprosy. He couldn't help but smile as she turned the corner and disappeared.

⚘

Throughout General Conference, the prophet and apostles left no doubt that the Saints needed to be prepared for major changes in their lives. One apostle explained that while each geographical area of the Church faced different circumstances, members of the Church should be ready if called upon to separate themselves from the world and gather together. The story of Lehi leading his family out of Jerusalem was mentioned in three separate talks.

Another apostle looked directly into the TV camera and said, "Eliminate any credit card debt, and live within your means. Set your lives in order so that you could leave your current situation at a moment's notice if the Lord asks. That time may soon come, and you must be free from the world's entanglements."

During the Priesthood Session the prophet strongly condemned the chip and told the men to avoid it like the plague. He also urged them to be more virtuous than they had ever been, explaining that they needed to be in tune with the Spirit in order to make wise choices in the coming weeks and months.

However, the climactic moment of General Conference came at the end of the Sunday afternoon session when the prophet announced, "All calls for proselyting missions are being indefinitely suspended. No young men or women will be called to serve as full-time missionaries for the foreseeable future, and all U.S.-born missionaries serving outside the United States will be returning home within two weeks. Senior couples who are serving at temples will continue their missions, but all other senior missionaries will be returning home."

The prophet paused, allowing the announcement to sink in, before adding, "This decision is in fulfillment of several prophecies, including one by Brigham Young, who taught, 'When the testimony of the Elders ceases to be given, and the Lord says to them, "Come home; I will now preach my own sermons to the nations of the earth," all you now know can scarcely be called a preface to the sermon that will be preached with fire and sword, tempests, earthquakes, hail, rain, thunders and lightnings, and fearful destruction.'"

The prophet looked steadily into the TV camera and said, "The perilous times that President Young spoke of are rapidly approaching, but the Lord will protect his righteous Saints. I admonish you to carefully ponder the words of counsel that have been given during this conference, and may God bless you all."

❧

Nathan and Chet were exhausted when they returned to their apartment that Sunday night, but they were excited by the tone of General Conference.

"I'll bet it won't be too long before the prophet's letter is sent," Chet said. "The apostles were clearly making a final plea for the Saints to turn their lives around."

"I agree," Nathan said. "You'd think the fact the Church is suspending proselyting calls and bringing missionaries home from overseas would be a big hint that changes are coming quickly."

Chet nodded. "Let's hope the Saints were listening."

CHAPTER 19

A month had passed since Dragon's departure from China. He'd taken a train across China into Europe, then switched to a car driven by one of his colleagues. They were always accompanied by at least two security agents. He wished they could just fly to their destination, but the risk was too great. They knew the Americans had uncovered some data about their mission, so it was better to just slowly make their way across the world and hide their trail.

They eventually reached Spain, where they boarded a Chinese merchant vessel. After enduring a stormy voyage across the Atlantic Ocean, Dragon now stood in the city of Freeport, Bahamas, only 65 miles off the coast of Florida.

The processing station in Freeport was owned and operated by the Chinese government, so Dragon merely flashed his ID badge as he passed through customs, and no one asked him about the briefcase handcuffed to his wrist. He was now clear to enter the United States without further inspection.

He was happy to be on dry land again, and he enjoyed a large lunch with a colleague who gave him an update on the status of the assignment, including the location in the United States where he would meet three other team members.

Within an hour he was aboard a large yacht that had been awaiting his arrival. By nightfall he set foot in Miami, Florida, where a bulletproof Chevy Tahoe whisked him to the West Palm Beach Marriott Hotel, where the others would meet him the next morning.

Once he was checked into his room under an assumed name,

Dragon finally unlocked the handcuff that had chained him to the briefcase ever since he left Beijing. He had become so accustomed to it that he actually felt troubled not having it attached to him, but he slipped it under the bed and said quietly, "Just one more day and this burden won't be mine alone."

❧

The next morning Dragon checked his watch. His partners were scheduled to arrive separately between 8 a.m. and 8:15 a.m. He was excited to see them again. Ten months earlier they had rehearsed this part of the plan—minus his deadly cargo. Last year's practice run had gone smoothly, but now the pressure was on.

Dragon didn't even know the actual names of the others—only their nicknames. This helped protect them if one of them happened to be captured. Even if they were tortured in an effort to extract information, they didn't have enough details about each other to derail the overall mission.

There was a long, unique knock on the door, and Dragon went to answer it. Through the eyehole he saw a clean-cut red-headed man.

"What's the capital of Florida?" Dragon asked loudly through the door.

"Fire."

Dragon nodded to himself. The answer itself was wrong, but the password—the man's nickname—was right. He unlocked the door and let the man enter. Within five minutes a Hispanic man known as Wind entered, and finally an African-American woman called Rain joined them.

"Dragon, it's good to see you again," Rain said. "You've got the cargo with you, right?"

"Yes, the scientists have made great improvements on the toxin's mixture, and we should have great success."

Dragon pulled the briefcase out from under the bed, then placed it on the room's small table. As he popped it open and revealed the four containers, the others watched silently.

"They don't look too threatening," Wind said. "I can't imagine anyone stopping us to inspect them."

"I agree," Dragon said, "but just in case, I went down the street to the 7-Eleven store and got Big Gulp cups—along with lids and straws—that we can hide them in."

"Good idea," Fire said.

After handing each partner a cup, Dragon carefully lifted each thermos container and placed it in a cup. Then he stuck the straw through the lid, ran it alongside the container and fastened the lid down on each one. The four partners paused and looked at each other, trying to fathom what their actions were going to unleash.

"I guess this is good-bye," Rain said.

Dragon nodded. "Our vehicles are waiting in the parking lot. Everything you need is in the trunk of your car, including plenty of cash for gas. I wish you success, so we can all enjoy the fruits of our mission."

The man known as Fire cleared his throat. "Speaking of that, you're sure the payment will be in my account at the end of the mission?"

"Yes," Dragon told him. "Once you fulfill your assignment, you'll each be financially set for the rest of your lives."

"Sounds good to me," Rain said. "Let's get the show on the road."

They carried their Big Gulp cups through the hotel lobby toward a row of Mazda sedans. Rain was heading north to New York City, while Wind had the most challenging assignment. He was on his way to Los Angeles to infiltrate the hospitals in the earthquake recovery zone and add to the troubles that were piling up in southern California.

Fire was also traveling to California, heading to San Francisco, but he'd be traveling along a different route as a security precaution.

Dragon waved as each of them pulled out of the parking lot and disappeared into traffic. Then he turned to signal his colleague who had been keeping watch on the cars. The others hadn't even noticed him.

"We're on our way," Dragon said as the man approached. "Please go retrieve the empty briefcase from the room and check me out of the hotel."

"Yes, sir," the man said. "Drive safely."

Dragon climbed into the Mazda, put the Big Gulp cup in the car's beverage holder, then exited the parking lot onto the road. Just as it had been strange to not have the briefcase handcuffed to his wrist, it was also peculiar to not have a bodyguard with him. This was the final stage now. Success or failure rested completely on the four partners.

Dragon sighed, feeling the weight of the assignment. It would be a long drive, but soon enough he would reach his destination—Salt Lake City, the so-called "Crossroads of the West."

CHAPTER 20

As April came to a close, the Church camps were well-stocked with food supplies. Nathan had put several thousand miles on his truck, delivering items to more than twenty different camps throughout the northern Rocky Mountains. In the past week he'd also been assigned to be part of a caravan of Church trucks that delivered food to earthquake victims in southern California, hoping it would reach those who needed it the most. They had dropped off the food at a Church meetinghouse in Victorville, which was on the eastern edge of the earthquake zone. While they were there, they talked to several people who said the government was downplaying the seriousness of the earthquake. They claimed some of the aftershocks had been nearly as bad as the initial quake, and that many more thousands of people had been killed in the disaster than the news media had reported.

When Nathan asked one man why the government wouldn't just tell the truth, the man shrugged and said, "I suppose they just don't want people to panic about it, but it's a madhouse in parts of L.A. The police are outnumbered and the rioting is out of control. That's why we're not taking these supplies any closer yet. We're at the point where the survivors are going to have to come to us, because we don't dare take it to them."

That conversation haunted Nathan on the drive back to Utah, but he knew it was another signal that the nation was teetering on the edge of chaos. During his daily drives, he'd taken the opportunity to work his way through audio versions of the Book of Mormon, the Doctrine & Covenants, and several recent General

Conferences. Now after the trip to California, he listened carefully for guidance and instructions to the Saints about the Last Days, and the references to "gathering" and "standing in holy places" had jumped out at him over and over. It was clear to him that the Lord fully intended to take care of his faithful Saints during the perilous times preceding his Second Coming.

Nearly all of his deliveries had been made to the so-called "white-sticker camps" where the Saints who first heeded the prophet's call would gather. Some of the camps were quite spacious, while a few were smaller and tucked away in side canyons. Each one he visited was high in the mountains, and even with detailed maps and directions, he often missed the well-hidden camp entrance and had to backtrack.

"If even *I* can't find the entrances, I'm pretty sure any troublemakers won't ether," he told himself.

On the last Monday of the month, Nathan and the other truck drivers were told they'd be working on a new assignment for a few days. Nathan's supervisor handed him a printout with an Orem address. Nathan read it and asked, "This address is on the west side of I-15, right?"

"Yes," the supervisor said. "Drive your truck to this location and you'll receive more instructions there."

That morning Nathan drove to the address listed on the paper and pulled up in front of an ordinary brown warehouse. He saw his roommate Chet already there, standing outside his truck.

"Why didn't they tell us we were going to the same place?" Nathan asked him.

"I don't know. I guess they don't like us looking like a convoy. Let's check it out."

There were a couple of cars parked near the entrance. Nathan tried opening the door, but it was locked, so he banged on it a couple of times. Within a few seconds a gray-haired man opened the door. "How may I help you?" he asked.

"We're here from the Bishop's Storehouse," Chet said. "They said if we came here we'd be given further details."

The man looked past them at their trucks. "Are those yours?"

Nathan nodded, and the man said, "Pull them around the side of the building and back up to the tallest garage doors. I'll meet you there."

As Nathan and Chet moved their trucks into position, the garage doors opened. They hopped out and were surprised by what they saw inside—hundreds of cardboard boxes labeled "Large canvas tents."

"This is the last step of the camp preparations," the man said. "We didn't want to take the tents to the camps too soon, because you'll be unloading them onto tarps out in the open. Now that spring is here they'll be fine until the Saints arrive to set them up."

"Where did all of these tents come from?" Nathan asked.

"The Church has been buying them 100 at a time, under the category of humanitarian aid," the man said. "Every Tuesday for the past two years an 18-wheeler has backed up to the dock and we've unloaded them."

Nathan did some quick math in his head. "So you have close to 10,000 tents in here?"

"Yes, and there's the same setup at warehouses in Logan and Cedar City, so the Church has bought a lot of tents! Now it's time for us to get them to the campsites."

As they spoke, a few other drivers arrived that Nathan recognized, and throughout the morning everyone pitched in to move the tents onto pallets so forklift operators could load them into the trucks. Nathan's truck could hold 60 boxes, and he took his first load to a distant camp near Park City before repeating the process twice more that day. He was grateful that several service missionaries were waiting to help him unload the tents, because his back was really starting to hurt.

By Wednesday night, the endless procession of trucks finally emptied out the three warehouses, and the tents were at their proper locations. Nathan was exhausted, and as he and Chet returned to their apartment, they hardly acknowledged each other before crashing into their beds.

A few minutes later, there was a knock on the door. Nathan groggily answered it, and one of their supervisors was standing there. He simply said, "Come to the storehouse at 8 a.m. wearing a suit and a tie. We've got a long day ahead of us."

Nathan relayed the news to Chet, who rolled over and said, "It couldn't possibly be longer than today was. I'll be dreaming about tent boxes all night."

CHAPTER 21

When Nathan and Chet arrived in their suits at the Bishop's Storehouse the next morning, they were directed to a conference room, where dozens of other maintenance missionaries were gathered. Nathan hadn't seen some of them since their first day of training together. There were several other men he'd never seen before, but he sensed they were also maintenance missionaries.

Elder Miller was at the front of the room, and he stood silently as numerous containers holding manila envelopes were placed on tables beside him. Once the tables were filled, he grabbed a microphone and faced the group.

"Today we shift gears," Elder Miller said excitedly. "The prophet received a revelation yesterday that the time has come to distribute the letters. You'll each be assigned to deliver letters to bishops in approximately three stakes somewhere along the Wasatch Front. You have two days to get these into their hands. It is absolutely essential that the bishop or one of his counselors receive the envelope and reads the message printed on the front. When you complete your task, return to this room and report directly to me."

"Are we allowed to know what the letter says?" one of the missionaries asked.

Elder Miller pondered the question for a moment, then nodded. "Yes, I feel that is fair. Of course, you're all bound to secrecy until the letters are read on Sunday in each ward."

He took a manila envelope from a table next to him and opened it. He said, "So you know, each letter is signed by the corresponding area presidency, and is tailored to the needs of that area."

He put on a pair of glasses and read:

"To the LDS Church members in the Utah South Area:

"In recent General Conference addresses and in several Ensign magazine articles, the First Presidency and the Quorum of the Twelve Apostles have given repeated warnings to both the nation and to the members of the Church. They have spoken of the need for spiritual and temporal preparedness in anticipation of upcoming events that will transpire if the commandments of God are ignored. These prophetic warnings have largely gone unheeded, and the Lord will soon fulfill his promises as outlined in the Doctrine and Covenants.

"Therefore, under the direction of the First Presidency, we issue an invitation of gathering to you. The Church has prepared gathering places along the Wasatch Front where members of the Church can be shielded from any turmoil that may soon come upon our nation. Your local leaders have been given specific instructions on where your particular stake has been assigned to gather.

"Sincerely,

"The Utah South Area Presidency"

Elder Miller put the letter back in the envelope and pulled out another sheet. "The bishops also will receive this list of instructions. They are told to read the letter at the start of Sacrament Meeting this coming Sunday, and then tell the members that a semi-trailer will be brought to their building that afternoon for families to bring their clothing and food storage. Then he'll tell them that the buses will be leaving for their camp that evening."

Chet raised his hand. "So the ward members only have a few hours to prepare? Why not give them a couple of days?"

Nathan knew Chet was purposely playing the devil's advocate, but Elder Miller's eyes narrowed.

"The Saints have been told specifically and repeatedly over the past few months to prepare, especially a few weeks ago at General Conference," he said. "Now comes the true test. Who will be ready for the Bridegroom?"

The reference to the Parable of the Ten Virgins was clear to everyone, and Chet nodded. "You're right," he said. "Either they're ready by now or they're not."

Elder Miller's stern look softened slightly. "If families choose not to leave their homes on Sunday, are they lost forever? No. But as we mentioned at the start of your assignment, the Saints who respond to the prophet's invitation will be taken to the best camps with the most supplies, safely tucked away from civilization. They'll be greatly blessed for their immediate obedience. Others might decide to come in a few days or weeks, but their opportunities will be greatly limited both temporally and spiritually compared to if they had obeyed promptly. As we've told you before, this is part of the Lord's larger plan to see who is truly faithful, and who is living on borrowed light each Sunday."

Elder Miller paused to collect his thoughts. "That reminds me of what President Ezra Taft Benson once said. It hit me so hard that I memorized it. He said, 'There is a real sifting going on in the Church, and it is going to become more pronounced with the passing of time. It will sift the wheat from the tares, because we face some difficult days, the like of which we have never experienced in our lives. And those days are going to require faith and testimony and family unity, the like of which we have never had.'"

The room was silent before he added, "Brethren, those days have arrived."

After a few more instructions, each maintenance missionary was given a stack of manila envelopes. Nathan's envelopes were all addressed to bishops in Spanish Fork, Utah. He was given a map of that city along with a clipboard and a pen where the recipient needed to sign that he had received the letter.

Nathan noticed each envelope had the official logo of the Church in the upper lefthand corner, and along the bottom of the envelope was printed: "*Urgent material that must be read by Friday, but do not open until you are in your office in the presence of your bishopric counselors.*"

"Why would they put that on there?" Nathan asked Chet, who was now standing near him.

"I think it's so there will be at least three witnesses that the letter was read. It's hard to believe, but there are some bishops who might choose to disregard the letter if it isn't first read in the presence of others."

"Can you fathom that?" Nathan asked. "If a bishop refused to read this to his congregation, he'd be potentially dooming his whole ward."

"Exactly. That's why there's so many double-checks."

Nathan was assigned a small Church-owned car, and it felt strange to be behind the wheel of this smaller car after so many weeks driving his truck. He zoomed down the freeway into southern Utah County and had to make a conscious effort to avoid speeding.

He arrived in Spanish Fork by early afternoon and had little trouble locating the bishops' houses, but only a few were home from work yet. Their wives or children offered to sign for them, but Nathan assured them that the bishop himself needed to receive it. He was usually able to arrange a time to return to the house, and once evening arrived, he made much better progress at getting the envelopes delivered.

In other cases, the bishop's family member said, "He's down at the church," and Nathan soon realized he could catch two or three bishops in one stop there. The bishops all seemed curious about the envelope and asked him why it was hand-delivered, but all he could do was point to the sentence printed on the front of the envelope.

By 9:30 p.m., he had delivered his last envelope and began driving back to Salt Lake. He arrived at the distribution center at 11 p.m., but he followed Elder Miller's instructions and went to the conference room. He was surprised to see Elder Miller still there, talking to other missionaries.

"Hi Nathan," Elder Miller said as he took the clipboard from him. "How did it go?"

"I delivered every one of them. Three bishops were out of town, but in each case I delivered the letter to one of the counselors."

"Excellent," Elder Miller said. "We'll have some of our senior missionaries call each person on this list on Saturday to make sure they've met as a bishopric and that they understand the letter."

"That's a good idea," Nathan said. "I'm sure they'll have plenty of questions."

Elder Miller patted him on the back. "Well done, my young friend. You've earned a good night's sleep."

"Thank you," Nathan said with a weary smile. "Do you think our pace will slow down soon?"

Elder Miller smiled back. "Only in your dreams. Sleep tight."

CHAPTER 22

On Sunday morning, Nathan parked a large bus in the far end of his meetinghouse's parking in Orem. He'd spent the past two days helping to retrieve buses throughout northern Utah that the Church had rented to take the Saints to the mountain refuges, so it was a relief to finally reach this point.

He'd been thrilled in their coordination meeting the day before at the Bishop's Storehouse when Elder Miller had said, "Whenever possible, we've assigned you to your home ward so you can encourage your family and friends to gather if they're hesitant about following the prophet's invitation. This is the most crucial decision they'll ever make."

"How much can we reveal to them?" Chet asked.

"Not much," Elder Miller said. "I recommend you simply tell them the same thing I've been telling my family—get on the bus. No matter what happens, get on the bus!"

There had been some conflict during that meeting, though, when Elder Miller told the missionaries they must ask each person boarding the bus whether they'd received the chip. If people had been implanted, they couldn't board the bus.

"Why not?" one missionary asked. "That doesn't seem very Christlike to me."

Elder Miller quickly turned on him, his face grim. "Our sources tell us the government is already tracking people's movements using their chip, and we can't risk having our camps discovered that way. Besides, wouldn't you agree the Church has clearly warned the Saints to never get the chip?"

"Yes, I do."

"Then is it fair to other Saints if their camp is discovered by the enemy because of someone's chip?"

The missionary was taken aback. "No, but that wouldn't—"

Elder Miller held up his hand. "Don't say it wouldn't happen! It will happen! Do you think all of this preparation by the Church is just for fun? We're in a spiritual war, and the chip is one of Satan's tactics. Evil forces are among us. It might not be fully evident yet, but it soon will be."

❧

After locking the bus, Nathan walked to the meetinghouse just before the start of Sacrament Meeting. As he entered the building he was greeted by several ward members. Everyone seemed cheerful and upbeat, but he knew their moods were about to change.

He took a seat toward the back of the chapel and looked around for Marie's parents, but they hadn't arrived yet. He turned his attention to the bishopric on the stand and noticed they were unusually somber as they watched the congregation take their seats.

Bishop Tanner made eye contact with Nathan, who gave him a small smile and a thumbs-up. The bishop was aware that Nathan was working in some capacity for the Church, and suddenly everything clicked in his mind.

"You know?" the bishop mouthed to Nathan, who nodded.

After the opening song and prayer, Bishop Tanner stepped to the pulpit holding a single sheet of paper.

"We have a special announcement today," he said. "I've been given a letter from our Area Presidency to read to the congregation. What it contains might come as a surprise to you, but I feel it is the will of the Lord and I'll follow these instructions."

Bishop Tanner then read the letter inviting the ward members to gather to a refuge in the mountains. As he read the letter, Nathan watched families begin whispering to each other, and some members appeared completely stunned.

Bishop Tanner finished reading the letter then said, "Our ward will be gathering with other stakes from Orem at a former girls camp in the mountains above Kamas, Utah. As the letter says, the gathering is taking place today. We've made copies of the letter and other instructions for every family in the ward, and we'll pass them out to you in the foyer. We ask that all the home teachers make sure your assigned families receive a copy if they aren't in attendance today."

The bishop continued, "We've been told to have you return to your homes at this time. There will be a semi-trailer brought to the Church this afternoon. All families who choose to gather with the stake should bring their food storage to the trailer. A bus will leave from this building at 5 p.m. to take us to the camp. Just so you know, this announcement is being made in wards all along the Wasatch Front and also in surrounding areas. We know this will be a difficult decision, but we know that if you ask the Lord in humility about this invitation from our leaders, you'll receive a confirmation about what you should do. I testify this is the Lord's will for us at this time, and I close this meeting in the name of Jesus Christ, Amen."

Bishop Tanner led his counselors off the stand and exited to the foyer. Conversations erupted all over the chapel, and everyone seemed unsure what to do. Eventually they started moving to the foyer to receive their copy of the letter.

Nathan noticed the Shaws were now standing in the back of the chapel, and he went toward them. Carol gave him a hug.

"Have you heard from Marie?" Nathan asked.

"Yes, and she seems to be doing well," Carol said.

"That's good, right?"

"That's all we can hope for," Aaron said. "How's your job with the Church going?"

"Good. I'm actually part of this gathering project that the bishop announced. I'll be the one driving the bus to the camp."

"Wow, you're right in the thick of it," Aaron said.

Nathan searched their faces. "So, are you two going to the mountain camp?"

They both looked at the ground for a moment. Aaron finally said, "We'll be staying for now. To be honest, I can't just leave my job that quickly. The government would get suspicious. Plus, if Marie came back, she wouldn't know where to find us."

Nathan was surprised at Aaron's answer. He was sure the Shaws would've been the first ones on the bus.

"I guess I can understand," he said. "I wish Marie was here as well. Please tell her hello from me when you talk with her."

"We will," Carol said. "Um, she said she tried to call you but couldn't get through. Your number was no longer in service."

"She really tried to reach me?" Nathan asked. "Tell her I'm sorry about our argument and that I'm eager to see her again. Hopefully this job won't last forever."

Carol smiled. "She'll be happy to hear that. Please don't give up on her. Hopefully this experience will help her appreciate the Church more."

"I'm hoping for that myself," Nathan said. "Well, I better get things coordinated with the bishop. If you change your mind, the bus is leaving at 5 p.m."

He shook Aaron's hand, and Carol gave him a quick embrace. "We care about you, Nathan. Stay out of danger!"

"You too," Nathan said before stepping away, fighting off the first real pangs of homesickness he'd felt in a long time.

❧

The rest of the day was a blur for him. He moved the bus closer to the meetinghouse, and soon a fellow maintenance missionary arrived in an 18-wheeler and unhitched the trailer next to the bus. Nathan stayed busy throughout the afternoon loading the trailer with food storage and other useful items that members were bringing from their homes.

The supplies from all three wards in the building were being put in the same trailer, and within a couple of hours two other buses arrived to transport members from the other wards that also met in the building.

As 5 p.m. approached, a line of people began to form on the curb alongside Nathan's bus. He stopped loading the trailer, opened the bus door, then stood on the first step.

"I'm happy to see you all here right on time," he said. "I want to assure you we're not just dropping you out into the wilderness to fend for yourselves. I've visited your camp location several times, and it's beautiful."

One lady near the front of the line raised her hand. "I'm eager to get there! I've been waiting a long time for this day."

Nathan smiled at her. "You knew this was coming?"

"Absolutely, and so did a lot of my friends. The Lord has been guiding us for several years to prepare for such an event."

"I agree with you," Nathan said.

Just then a minivan pulled into the parking lot, and an older couple let out cries of relief as a woman and her three young children hurried toward them. The man walked toward Nathan and said, "This is my daughter and her kids from Pleasant Grove. She's a single mom, and she really wants to be with us. Would it be all right if they come to our camp?"

Elder Miller had discussed this possibility with the missionaries, and he'd said if extended families felt inspired to be in the same camp, it would be okay.

"Yes," Nathan said. "The more the merrier."

The man thanked him profusely, and the couple embraced their daughter while the others in line welcomed the new arrivals.

Nathan took a clipboard that held a list of current ward members and began checking people onto the bus. He asked each person if they had received the government's microchip, and most simply said, "No."

However, one feisty woman said, "Most certainly not! Besides, why would anyone who got the chip want to go to the camp? They already disobeyed the prophet once, right?"

Nathan raised his eyebrows. "I can't argue with that."

By 5:20 the bus was mostly full, but there were still a few seats left. Nathan checked in the last family and then looked through the list. There were about 60 people on board. As he looked at their faces, he wasn't surprised to see many longtime stalwarts of the ward. It saddened him, though, that only six families with younger children were on the bus.

The other two buses soon departed, and Nathan motioned to Bishop Tanner, who was sitting with his family in one of the front seats. The bishop came forward, and Nathan' handed him the clipboard. "Please look through this list and see if you expect anyone else to come."

The bishop glanced through the names, shaking his head a few times. "Wow, there's quite a few more that I thought would be here—including our ward clerk and his family—but I suppose we need to leave, right?"

Nathan shrugged. "The other buses have left, but I'll wait as long as you want. I think we should get to the camp while there's still some daylight, though."

Bishop Tanner nodded as he peered out the front window of the bus looking in vain for more arrivals. "That's fine. They knew what time we were leaving."

"Very well," Nathan said. "Let me shut the trailer."

He hopped out of the bus and locked the semi-trailer that his colleague would retrieve that evening and take to the camp the next day. He was pleased to see it was filled with all kinds of cans and boxes. It would be a nice addition to the supplies he had already delivered to the camp during the past few weeks.

Nathan stepped back into the bus, and Bishop Tanner said, "While you were locking the trailer, I told the group that I'd like to leave with a prayer."

"I think that's wonderful."

The bishop faced the bus passengers and offered a tremendous prayer that was filled with gratitude for their many blessings. Nathan felt the Spirit descend on the bus, and he sensed angels were already watching over them.

Soon they were traveling along 800 North in Orem heading toward Provo Canyon. The bus passengers were silent as they stared out the windows to take one last look at their hometown. They passed two other churches, where semi-trailers sat waiting for the maintenance missionaries to retrieve them. Otherwise, everyday life continued on, with people taking walks or riding bikes on the sidewalk. A few people even waved as the bus passed by.

As the bus entered Provo Canyon, the group seemed to let out a collective sigh of relief. Nathan smiled to himself as he heard one woman say, "I figured if Lehi's wife Sariah could leave her home in Jerusalem, then so could I. The Lord giveth and the Lord taketh away. Blessed be the name of the Lord."

"Amen," Nathan whispered.

৯৯

They arrived at the camp with just a few minutes of sunlight to spare, but several other wards had already arrived and were making great progress on setting up the tents. Everyone pitched in to help in some way, and within a few minutes Nathan felt confident he could leave the group in the hands of the senior missionaries who were there. He found Bishop Tanner and shook his hand. "

"It looks like you're in great shape here," Nathan said. "I better start back down the canyon and return the bus to Salt Lake, but I'll be thinking of you."

Bishop Tanner clasped his shoulder and said, "Thank you, Nathan. I know you'll be busy, but please check in on our other ward members once in a while if you can. I'm elated to be here, but it breaks my heart that only a small percentage of the ward choose to accept the prophet's invitation. I can't believe the Shaws didn't come."

"Me too, but I think they're worried about Marie," Nathan said. "But I'll keep an eye out for them and others in the neighborhood. I'm even going to give my dad a try."

The bishop's eyes got misty. "They're good people, but they've allowed worldly things to block the Spirit from their lives."

Nathan bid farewell to a few other ward members, then he headed down the canyon. He pondered the events of that day and realized America had reached a key point in history. The Lord's faithful Saints were safely tucked away in protected refuges, and now the Lord would fulfill his own decrees. The words of D&C 45:32-33 came into Nathan's mind:

"But my disciples shall stand in holy places, and shall not be moved; but among the wicked, men shall lift up their voices and curse God and die. And there shall be earthquakes also in divers places, and many desolations; yet men will harden their hearts against me, and they will take up the sword, one against another, and they will kill one another."

Nathan shuddered, knowing the California earthquake was likely the start of many similar catastrophes across the nation.

"Oh, Marie," Nathan said. "Please come home."

CHAPTER 23

Marie was enjoying her internship in Chicago, but Gretchen was keeping her so busy that Sunday was really her only day off. She'd been sleeping in each Sunday to rejuvenate herself. She hadn't attended church yet and actually didn't know where the closest meetinghouse was.

She felt mildly guilty about it, but she really needed a mental break each week, rather than having more people tell her what she should do. She really admired Gretchen, but the woman never slowed down. It was always "rush, rush, rush" with her.

It was a beautiful Sabbath morning, so Marie put on some casual clothes and decided to do some exploring. The Bloomingdale's Building had literally everything she needed, so she had rarely gone outside.

"Go get some sunshine," she told herself.

She purposely left her cell phone on the kitchen counter and made her way down to Michigan Avenue. The sidewalk was relatively empty, so she just started walking south along the Magnificent Mile. After a half hour she decided to get her first close-up look at Lake Michigan and she made her way to Navy Pier.

She walked among the crowds there, just blending in, and occasionally going to the edge of the pier to feel the soft breeze on her face. She stood beneath the huge Ferris Wheel that dominated the sky and felt liberated, realizing no one on earth knew where she was at that moment.

As Marie began to leave the pier, she walked alongside a convention center known as Festival Hall. On one of the lower levels she saw a sign that read "The Smith Museum of Stained Glass Windows." She noticed admission was free, and she figured it was a good way to spend Sunday. She was pleased that many of the windows depicted the Savior, and she felt spiritually refreshed as she studied each window.

"Heavenly Father, I'm going to church next Sunday, no matter what," she prayed as she left the museum.

She'd enjoyed her time wandering the city so much that she dreaded going back to her apartment, but the sun would be setting soon and she remembered Bianca's counsel about being alone on the streets after dark.

She returned to her apartment to find her parents had left a phone message. She checked the message and heard her mother say, "Marie, we need to talk to you. Call us as soon as you get this."

Marie called them back and was surprised at how relieved they sounded to hear her voice. Carol got on one line and Aaron got on another one so they could all talk together.

"Did you hear the announcement in Church today?" Carol asked.

"Uh, no. I didn't make it there. What happened?"

"The prophet invited all of the Church members to gather to camps in the mountains. It's causing quite a stir around here."

Marie paused. "I guess I'm confused. Why would the prophet ask us to do this? Are things really that bad?"

"Not at this moment, but everything could fall apart quickly."

"Are you two going to a camp?" Marie asked.

"Not yet," Aaron said. "It would be impossible to leave my job that quickly. But we plan to, and hopefully you'll come with us."

"I don't know about that," Marie said. "It still seems to be some sort of knee-jerk reaction. Let me think about it."

"By the way, we saw Nathan this morning," Aaron said. "Part of his job is to help transport people to the camps. He wanted us to tell you hello and that he's eager to see you again."

Marie's heart skipped a beat. "I want to see him, too. I admit I'm feeling a little lonely."

"Is there any chance you could fly home for a weekend?" Carol asked. "We'd be happy to pay for it."

"I wish I could, but they have assignments lined out for me several weeks in advance. I feel like I'm running as fast as I can but that I'm falling even more behind."

"Are they treating you okay?" Aaron asked.

"Yes, and they're very happy with me. I'm just still adjusting to the pace. Today I just needed some time alone, so I took a nice walk down to a pier on Lake Michigan, and I feel like myself again."

"That's good to hear," Carol said. "Is there anything else we can do for you?"

"Just make the next three months go faster," Marie said with a laugh. "I miss home, but I'm going to stick it out."

They talked for a few more minutes, but after they hung up, all she could think about was that Nathan was eager to see her again. His absence had indeed made her heart grow fonder, and she appreciated his high standards and values more than ever.

She'd agreed to go to a nightclub with Bianca that first weekend, but she had hated it. None of the men there came anywhere close to matching Nathan—in fact, they were somewhat revolting. Since then, Gretchen had dumped so much work on her that she'd had no trouble at all telling Bianca she needed to find a new designated driver.

❧

After talking with her parents, Marie took a long shower and got ready for bed in preparation for another long Monday, but she decided to check the local TV news to see if the Church's invitation to go to the camps was of interest to anyone. She was surprised to see it was the lead story with the caption "*Where Did All The Mormons Go?*" A woman was being interviewed by a reporter in front of the Chicago Temple.

"It's like the prophet went nuts or something," the woman said. "My neighbor knocked on my door and gave me a letter telling me to go live in the wilderness. I've never heard of such a thing, so I came down here to the temple to find out what's going on, but the place seems empty!"

The reporter nodded gravely. "So your church has never taught such things before? This just came out of the blue?"

"Exactly," the woman said as she adjusted her tanktop. "I'd love for someone to show me in the scriptures where people just take off for the hills on a moment's notice. It's insane!"

The reporter turned to the camera and said, "There you go. It looks like the Mormons have flown the cuckoo's nest, so to speak. Back to you in the studio."

Marie shook her head and turned off the TV.

"That woman's an idiot," she muttered. "She didn't even know the temple is closed on Sunday."

Marie fumed for a few minutes, but she was admittedly feeling apprehensive about the Saints being told by the prophet to gather in the mountains. She cringed as she remembered her parting words to Nathan—"*I highly doubt the world is going to collapse during my four months in Chicago.*"

Marie suddenly felt weak in the knees, but assured herself, "Everything is going to be all right. I just walked all over this city and had one of the most peaceful days of my life."

☙

The next morning Gretchen called Marie into her office and motioned toward a chair.

"I saw on the news that the Mormons have staged a mass evacuation," Gretchen said. "Are you planning to join them?"

Marie shook her head. "No, I'll be staying right here. It was just a small minority of our members. I'm not quite sure what's going on, but I talked to my parents, and they didn't go either."

"I'm glad to hear that. It seems really bizarre."

"It surprised me, too," Marie said. "Don't worry, I'll fulfill all of my internship duties."

"Thank you. You're doing a wonderful job. The ideas you've come up with are brilliant."

Marie smiled. "That means so much to me to hear you say that. I'm doing the best I can."

Gretchen waved her hand. "Sorry to question you about your religious beliefs. They're your own business. I just wanted to make sure I wasn't going to have to hire a new intern."

"Nope, I'm staying."

"Good," Gretchen said before holding up the front page of the *Chicago Sun-Times* that had been on her desk. Next to the article about the Mormons was one about a massive hurricane that was pummeling Central America. Gretchen added, "Maybe your prophet is afraid this hurricane is coming our way."

Marie peered with interest at the page. "Maybe so."

❦

During lunch Marie went on the internet and opened her favorite website, www.weather.com. She'd been so busy with her internship assignments that she hadn't checked the site for nearly two weeks, but Marie had always been fascinated by extreme weather, particularly hurricanes.

She'd been a young girl when Hurricane Katrina had hit the Gulf Coast in 2005, and that storm had damaged several homes owned by her mother's family in Mississippi. Her mom had talked about the hurricane non-stop for a couple of weeks after that, and since then, Marie had been a weather buff.

The lead story on the website was about Hurricane Barton, which had formed south of Cuba before heading west and thrashing Guatemala as a Category 5 storm with winds approaching 160 miles per hour, one of the strongest storms on record.

Marie clicked on a link that showed news footage taken along the Guatemalan coast and was stunned as she watched villages being flooded and torn apart.

"That's crazy," Marie said, as she clicked on a link to see where the storm might be headed. The hurricane experts were predicting five possible tracks the storm could take, including one where the storm would cross Mexico and then die out in the Pacific Ocean. However, one scenario had the storm turning north into the Gulf of Mexico and retaining its strength as it approached the coasts of Texas, Louisiana, and Mississippi.

"I hope that one's wrong," Marie whispered. "It could be Katrina all over again."

CHAPTER 24

By early May, Chinese diplomat Chen Ming—known to his associates as Dragon—had been in Salt Lake City for a full week. His only hint of trouble during his long drive from Florida was being pulled over by a highway patrolman late one night on Interstate 20 near Dallas, Texas.

When he saw the patrol car's lights flashing behind him, he glanced down and saw he was going 82 miles an hour. He cursed at himself for such a foolish mistake, but put on a pleasant smile as the officer approached his car.

"Hello, officer," Dragon said. "I just realized how fast I was going. Sorry about that."

The officer's stern look softened a little. "Let's take a look at your license and registration."

Dragon sat nervously as he waited for the officer to return, but he knew his colleagues in the Chinese Embassy had triple-checked everything related to his driver's license and the car. His record should now be spotless, despite three fender benders and a speeding ticket during his years working in Washington, D.C.

"You're good to go," the patrolman had told him when he brought the license back. "Just slow down a little, all right?"

"I will. Thank you, sir."

The officer then pointed to the Big Gulp cup resting in its dashboard holder. "That's just soda in there, right?"

"Of course, sir. No drinking and driving for me!"

As Dragon spent each night in his Salt Lake hotel room, he often reflected on his role in the upcoming overthrow of the United States. He knew his work at the Chinese Embassy in Washington, D.C. had been just a small piece in a large puzzle, but this bioterror mission was the first of many dominos that would help the Coalition nations eliminate America and Israel.

The Russians had been in favor of surprising the Americans with a full-scale military attack, but the Chinese leaders finally convinced their Coalition allies that a low-key and essentially invisible first attack would have a greater effect. Such an attack would greatly weaken America's resolve before the Coalition eventually followed through with Russia's wishes for a military invasion.

The Chinese took history as their guide. Attacks on America such as Japan's bombing of Pearl Harbor in 1941 and Osama bin Laden's toppling of the Twin Towers in 2001 had temporarily hurt the United States, but those events had also unified the Americans and in the end lifted their patriotism to greater heights.

Therefore, the Chinese plan would strike at the heart of America by causing disorder rather than unity. If everything went as expected, the U.S. economy would quickly unravel and never recover.

This first phase of the plan had been greatly aided in 2011 when Dutch scientists created a highly-contagious and deadly airborne mutation of the H5N1 flu virus. The scientists spent 2012 loudly proclaiming that their version of the virus wasn't as deadly as previously reported, but that didn't matter, because by then Chinese agents had already snuck into their laboratory and stolen a sample.

Over the next several months, a team of Coalition scientists was able to mutate the Dutch strain a step further, making it even more transferable and lethal. Then Chinese agents were able to obtain vials of the 1918 flu virus, which was added to the mix, along with a few other deadly illnesses. The final potion was the most potent human-killer the world had ever seen.

The toxin had been tested on humans under controlled

circumstances, and the mortality rate had been stunningly high. Dragon had seen time-lapse videos of prison inmates who had simply touched a sink where the mixture had been applied, and the effects on the human body were startling.

The Chinese scientists had nicknamed the resulting illness the "Black Flu" because it turned people's skin dark and caused intense flu-like symptoms. Victims often literally drowned from fluid in their lungs within hours, because the virus acted too quickly for the immune system to mount an effective defense. The only way America could avoid having the illness wipe out millions of their citizens was through a complete quarantine.

"That's just not going to happen," Dragon thought.

Dragon's father had been one of the original Chinese representatives as the Coalition was formed. By the 1990s when Dragon became a full-fledged member of the group, the plan was fully underway. Very few American leaders questioned China and Russia's rapid military growth during the early 21st century, and the plan proceeded smoothly and with great secrecy.

However, the Coalition leaders held their breaths in 2005 when a speech by Chi Haotian, the Vice-Chairman of China's Military Commission, was leaked onto the internet. Among other things, he revealed that China would "clean up" America through bioterrorism. He was quoted as saying, "It is indeed brutal to kill one or two hundred million Americans. But that is the only path that will secure a Chinese century, a century in which the CCP leads the world."

He added that the remaining Americans would serve as slaves while the Chinese kept the basic U.S. infrastructure intact. The Chinese braced for a public outcry, but his comments were basically ignored by America's media.

Actually, the Chinese hadn't expected to implement this part of the plan for several more years, but the Americans themselves had sped up the process through their own foolishness. Their national debt problem had suddenly exploded, and now China was suddenly worried the United States wouldn't be able to pay back what they had borrowed.

In some ways, the Chinese felt like the U.S. government was actually working in their best interest. The Chinese were astonished as America's leaders stifled capitalism at seemingly every turn. Meanwhile, a growing number of Americans seemed content to live "on the dole" so to speak, but the Chinese knew it wouldn't take much to tip this welfare state upside down.

Dragon smiled, knowing the tipping point would be triggered by the mixture in the Big Gulp cup sitting on his hotel table.

⌒

During his first day in Salt Lake, Dragon had scouted out several great locations to unleash his toxin. A key reason Salt Lake City was chosen was because Interstate 15 and Interstate 80 crossed there, and travelers would carry the illness in all directions.

He immediately considered the LDS Church's Temple Square as an obvious target, but on the day he walked past it, a group of men were cleaning graffiti off the outside wall. By the next day, a 12-foot-high metal fence had been placed around Temple Square as well as the blocks that held the Conference Center, the Joseph Smith Building and the Church Office Building.

"So much for that," he told himself. "I think Energy Solutions Arena is now the best location for widespread success."

That afternoon he had slipped into the arena and found a custodian mopping the floor. He saw her name on her shirt and said, "Hey Jasmine, I'm new in town and really need a job," Dragon told her. "I'll even clean toilets for free for a week just to show you what a good worker I am."

The woman raised her eyebrows. "You'd really do that?"

"Absolutely."

"Let's go talk to my supervisor," she said.

Within twenty minutes Dragon had been accepted as a volunteer worker—with the possibility of being hired in the future. He thanked the supervisor profusely, and Jasmine led him back to the custodian closet to give him a list of tasks she preferred not to do. Dragon spent the afternoon cleaning the urinals in all of the men's restrooms. Things couldn't have worked out better.

That evening he paid cash for a disposable cell phone and called his three other partners to find out how things were going for them. Rain reported she had taken a job at a concession stand in Madison Square Garden that gave her access to their nacho cheese and hot dog condiments.

"That will be great," Dragon told her. "If you can mix a little into the food, you'll have amazing results."

He then called Fire, who reported he'd been hired to move equipment for trade shows into the Moscone Center, San Francisco's largest convention complex. This job gave him access to all of the public areas, and with several big trade shows coming up, he was excited about his ability to spread the illness.

Meanwhile, Wind had faced the most challenging assignment due to the massive earthquake in southern California, and he didn't answer Dragon's initial call, but he later called to say he was able secure a spot as a volunteer at the Staples Center in Los Angeles, which had been turned into a shelter for those who had lost their homes.

"I work at a table handing out sheets and pillows, and my supposedly sanitary gloves will be covered with the toxin," he said. "This place will be a powderkeg within a couple of days."

"Excellent," Dragon told him. "Go ahead and get started. The rest of us will soon be underway as well."

While working the next day, Dragon noticed Energy Solutions Arena had events scheduled on three consecutive nights later in the week. Since the toxin would be most effective during the first 48 hours it was released, he'd be able to infect two diverse crowds who would travel back to their home cities and multiply the possible exposures before anyone realized what was happening. The toxin would probably be fading by the third night, but any additional infections would be a plus.

"It's hard to beat the diversity of pro wrestling, country music, and a Rolling Stones concert," Dragon said with a laugh. "Maybe we've finally found something that will finish off Mick Jagger."

Dragon became acquainted with a few other custodians, and all they wanted to talk about was Hurricane Barton. The storm had roared along the western edge of the Gulf of Mexico and had disabled or destroyed most of the oil rigs in its path. It was now bearing down on the Gulf Coast and mandatory evacuations were being ordered for millions of residents in Texas and Louisiana.

Dragon couldn't believe his luck. The American people would be so focused on the hurricane and the continuing earthquake recovery efforts in southern California that they wouldn't even be aware they were being hit by the worst bioterror attack in history.

The timing was perfect.

CHAPTER 25

⎯⎯⎯⎯⎯⎯ ❧ ⎯⎯⎯⎯⎯⎯

As word spread in the media that "the Mormons" had gone to hide in the mountains, vandals and looters took the opportunity to focus on Church buildings. Some meetinghouses were broken into then burned, while others were simply covered with graffiti.

The temples were being guarded by armed volunteers, but that didn't stop one group of vandals from overwhelming the guards at the Jordan River Temple and starting it on fire. The Church immediately closed all of the temples and locked the gates, then put the maintenance missionaries on full-time duty assembling a chainlink fence around Temple Square and the other Church-owned buildings on the surrounding blocks. The fence included a strand of electrified wire along the top to greet anyone who tried to climb it.

The missionaries then divided into 12-man teams and traveled throughout Utah and Idaho to fence off the other temples that weren't already being used as refuges. Nathan's team worked their way south, and finally they reached the St. George Temple. As he and Chet were securing the fencing across the temple's main entrance, a couple approached them dressed in Sunday clothes.

"What are you doing?" the woman asked angrily.

"Sorry, the temple is closed," Nathan said.

"What do you mean?" she asked. "We've been coming to the temple on the last Wednesday of the month for the past ten years. We need to keep our streak alive."

Chet was standing by, fastening the chainlink to a metal post. "Look around," he said. "Doesn't the empty parking lot tip you off

123

that things have changed? The temple workers have gone to the Church camps—where you should be."

The woman looked offended and turned to her husband. "Erik, are you going to let him talk to me that way?"

Erik just frowned. "He's right, Donna. We should've gone to the refuge with the ward."

Donna stamped her foot. "There's no way I'm going to live in a tent!"

Erik smiled tiredly at Nathan and Chet. "You two keep up the good work. You've helped me make up my mind. Which camp should I go to?"

"I'd recommend driving to the camp in Snow Canyon," Chet said. "They're still taking Saints there."

"Thank you," Erik said as he turned to his wife. "Come on, dear. Let's do the right thing and rejoin the Saints."

Donna looked shocked. "Are you serious?"

Erik gave a weary shrug. "I'm going. It's up to you whether you come along with me."

He started walking back to the car, and Donna followed, shouting at him all the way.

Chet chuckled. "I know I shouldn't laugh, but I pity him. I wonder if he's secretly hoping she chooses to stay behind."

❧

While Nathan and his team members were finishing the fencing job at the St. George Temple, they received a message to return to the Bishop's Storehouse in Salt Lake as quickly as possible for an emergency meeting. They drove back to Salt Lake and were bothered to see government vehicles setting up checkpoints along I-15.

"That doesn't look good," Chet said. "Something is definitely going on."

They arrived that evening at the Bishop's Storehouse, and Samuel was waiting for them at the door.

"I'm glad you guys made it," he said. "Elder Miller waited as long as he could, but the meeting is already underway. Go right in."

Their team slipped into the back of the room as Elder Miller thanked the missionaries for their diligent service. "Sometimes it is hard to believe there are only 300 of you," he said. "You've accomplished many amazing tasks. The prophet wishes he could personally thank you for all you've done."

Chet raised his hand hesitantly. "Sorry we're late, but it sounds like you're releasing us. Does this mean we're done?"

Elder Miller chuckled. "Not even close. But the nature of your service is going to change. Let me explain why. Apparently the Saints' departure to the camps has angered several top government officials. They're frustrated they can't trace the Saints, since none of them have the chip. So now with these natural disasters causing people to relocate, the government is going to use the excuse that they need to know where every citizen is as a matter of national security."

"How will they ever enforce that?" a missionary asked.

Nathan spoke up. "They were starting to set up checkpoints along the freeway even as we were coming back."

Yes, they're acting quickly," Elder Miller said. "They've already formed the Chip Compliance Agency, and their employees are going to start visiting homes and businesses as soon as tomorrow. If they find someone who doesn't have the chip, the person will be detained and be given two options—either be taken directly to a chip implantation center or be jailed indefinitely."

"What does that mean for us?" another missionary asked. "We won't be able to travel very easily."

Elder Miller paced the floor. "Your new assignment is to stay among the people, seeking out any good-hearted people before even greater troubles begin. You'll need to essentially make yourselves invisible. As the Spirit guides you, warn people about what is coming and encourage them to travel to one of our 'blue camps' and seek safety. Please double-check our map before you leave so you're familiar with where these camps are."

"Where should we start?" one of the missionaries asked. "Are you going to assign us to specific cities?"

"No. You're on your own, but I would suggest you go to your home wards and neighborhoods and see if you can get anyone who is still there to listen to you."

"Are the previous wards even recognized by the Church now?" Chet asked.

Elder Miller shrugged. "I don't want to say we don't care about them, but the focus now is on organizing new wards and stakes at the Church camps, rather than keeping the old wards staffed and operating."

"That makes sense," Chet said. "The members who are still here rejected the prophet's counsel."

"That's right," Elder Miller said. "They don't have the Spirit with them. We've already heard of wards that have 'elected' a new bishop. This isn't surprising. When the Saints left Nauvoo, some members stayed behind, but their wards either fell apart or they started their own version of the Church. The same thing is starting to happen here, but with the government putting pressure on all of the Christian churches, I think most of these members will just quit claiming to be Mormons."

"How has the Church been handling the government's harassment?" a missionary asked.

"We've been somewhat cooperative, but they're putting extreme pressure on the Church to reveal where the Saints are. The government is paranoid we're putting together a resistance force. Yesterday we were informed they might freeze our assets and seize our buildings and vehicles, which is what we've expected all along. The prophet and apostles are going to spread out, but they will still be leading the Church. Don't worry, we'll make it through this dark time and emerge triumphant."

The missionaries weren't quite so optimistic. "Will there be anyplace we can go if we're in danger?" one asked.

"Yes, we've established a password that will grant you access to the temple compounds and the refuges. It's quite simple. Go to an entrance and state, 'D&C 4:7.' The guard will then say, 'Proceed.' Then what will you tell him?"

Nathan raised his hand. "Ask, and ye shall receive; knock, and it shall be opened unto you. Amen."

"Correct," Elder Miller said. "Once you say 'Amen' he'll let you in. Simple enough?"

The missionaries all nodded.

Elder Miller looked across the room at the valiant servants of the Lord that he'd grown to love so much. "Like I've told you before, we're in a spiritual war," he said. "Just follow the Spirit and ask yourself, 'What would the Three Nephites do?'"

That comment brought smiles to the missionaries' faces.

"All kidding aside, use your priesthood power as you feel inspired to do so, whether to heal the sick or to defend yourself against evil. The Lord will grant you the righteous desires of your heart."

Elder Miller paused, suddenly overcome with emotion. "You've become like sons to me, and I'm so grateful to know each of you. Now go collect your belongings from your apartments, then we'll give you one final bus ride to the destination of your choice. Farewell, my dear brethren, until we meet again in a better time and place."

❧

Nathan joined several missionaries who were transported to Utah County, and he had the bus driver drop him off on the corner near the Shaws' home. He initially planned to first visit his father, but as the bus approached Orem, he felt compelled to see if Marie's parents were still in the city.

He knocked on the door and was relieved when Aaron opened it. He stepped forward and took Nathan by the arm. "Let's go for a walk, okay?"

Nathan shrugged. "That's fine with me."

Once they were moving down the sidewalk, Aaron said, "Sorry about that, but I think the government is bugging my house."

"Why would they do that?"

Aaron looked around, then said quietly, "For a very good reason. You and I are on the same team. I work at the NSA Data Center, but I also work undercover for the Church."

Nathan's eyes grew wide. "You're a double-agent?"

Aaron smiled. "I suppose, but I like to think of myself more like the spies that Alma and Captain Moroni used. I just relay information to the leaders of the Church about situations or government decisions that might affect them."

"Wow, you're in a precarious position."

"You're not kidding," Aaron said. "I fully realize that if the government finds out what I'm doing, they'll execute me immediately. But just like you, I feel I've got heavenly forces watching over me."

"That explains why you and Carol didn't go to the Kamas camp with the ward," Nathan said. "I was surprised you stayed behind, but now it makes sense."

"Yes, the Church leaders want me to stay right where I'm at. I had to get the chip after this latest push by the government, but I'm prepared to cut it out of my hand the moment I can head for the hills."

"Do the people you work with at the data center suspect anything?" Nathan asked.

"Well, I don't mention my religion at work, but ever since the Saints went to the refuges, my superiors have treated me differently. That's why I think the house is bugged. One day last week Carol came home and noticed items in the living room were positioned just a little differently than when she left, including the computer. So we don't use it much anymore. We searched the whole house for a bug, but we didn't find anything. Unfortunately, the incident has freaked Carol out, so she's been spending a lot of time out of the house."

"Have you talked to Marie lately?" Nathan asked.

"Yes, and I think she's ready to come home, but her stubborn streak won't let her admit it. She's determined to stick it out until the end of the internship."

"I just worry about her," Nathan said. "Elder Miller makes it sound like America is about to fall apart."

Aaron frowned. "He's right. I've often heard our country described as a raft on a river. We've had a fairly smooth ride for more than 230 years, but the canyon walls are narrowing and the rapids are more severe. We're right at the point where we could still paddle to the river bank and save ourselves, but I honestly believe the raft is now out of the citizens' control."

"I completely agree with you," Nathan said.

"The biggest problem is there's a huge waterfall downstream, and we're heading right for it," Aaron said. "The California earthquake and now the hurricane are stretching our country's resources to the limit, and I think we're heading for martial law if anything else bad happens. That's why the Lord removed his faithful Saints from society. They'll be spared from the turmoil that's coming. Have you heard about the Chip Compliance Authority?"

"Yes. Elder Miller told us about it just this morning."

"It's terrible," Aaron said. "Americans have no idea how closely their actions are being tracked. Now that the CCA is fully underway, they're going to start cracking down on anything out of the ordinary."

"What do they consider being out of the ordinary?"

Aaron shook his head in disgust. "Pretty much anything that would've been considered patriotic or Christian thirty years ago. Everything we believe in is being trampled on."

They had walked around the block and were back in front of Aaron's home. Nathan quickly explained his new role, and Aaron said, "Well, stop by when you can. The way things are going, we both might be heading to Kamas soon just to save ourselves."

CHAPTER 26

The day Dragon had selected for releasing his toxin finally arrived. He went to Energy Solutions Arena once again, just as he had for the past three days, cleaning toilets for free. This time, however, he took along a plastic bag that held high-quality rubber gloves, a protective mask, and a Big Gulp cup.

He went to a custodian closet, retrieved a pail and a sponge, then went to the nearest men's restroom. He pulled on the gloves and the mask, then took the lid off the Big Gulp cup and gently pulled the metallic canister out.

"At last," Dragon muttered as he twisted the lid open to reveal a goopy mixture that could have been mistaken for a grape Slurpee.

He carefully poured a portion into the pail, then added a gallon of water from a sink. He dipped a rag into the water and then began to wipe down the sink handles and toilet seats. He repeated the process in the adjoining women's restroom, then worked his way around the entire concourse.

He found an open door to the main arena, where a crew was putting the finishing touches on the stage for that night's pro wresting event. He dipped the rag once again in the water and began to slide it down a railing toward the stage.

"Hey, what are you doing?" a woman's voice rang out.

Dragon jerked around in surprise. It was Jasmine Bradley, the woman who had agreed to let him clean the toilets.

"Uh, hello Jasmine," Dragon said. "I finished cleaning the restrooms, so I thought I'd clean up in here. I heard someone threw up in this area last night. I'm just sanitizing everything."

Jasmine gave him a funny look. "Who told you that? We didn't have an event here last night."

Dragon acted surprised. "Really? Oh well. By the way, have you been happy with how I've been doing this week?"

"Yes, but you can't just roam around the building. You need to stay where you're assigned for security reasons." Jasmine stepped closer and looked into the pail. "Whoa, that water is filthy. Go change it out immediately and get back to cleaning the restrooms."

"You're right," Dragon said, looking into the pail. He slipped past her and headed down the concourse to the custodian closet where he had stashed the canister. Once he was inside the closet, rather than emptying the pail he dumped more of the toxin into it and got ready to sneak back into the arena. However, as he turned to leave the closet, he came face to face with Jasmine.

"I need to know exactly what's going on here," she said angrily. "What were you pouring into the bucket?"

Dragon couldn't believe this was happening. In an instant he grabbed her around the neck and slammed her head into the wall. As she cried out in pain, he smashed his fist into her temple, causing her to slump unconscious to the floor.

Dragon quickly stepped over her and shut the closet door behind him. He knew there were security cameras throughout the concourse, so he casually walked to the nearest exit and back to his hotel, not wanting to draw attention to himself.

He soon entered his hotel room and let out a sigh of relief. He changed out of his custodian uniform and stuffed them into a suitcase before changing into business attire, He then parted the room's curtains, which gave him a decent view of the street in front of Energy Solutions Arena. He paced back and forth, knowing he'd made a foolish mistake by leaving the canister behind. He desperately wanted to retrieve it, but he sensed doing so would only lead to him receiving a long prison sentence.

"Why did I go into the arena?" he cried out. "I was basically done with the job. Those restrooms are going to be toxic for several days and thousands would have died."

Moments later the first police car came screaming down the street, followed by six other emergency vehicles. They all squealed to a stop in front of the arena. A few people then climbed out of a van in protective suits.

"They found the toxin," he thought.

Dragon knew he needed to leave the area immediately, but he couldn't take his eyes off the drama that was unfolding. Dragon saw someone being carried out of the building on a stretcher and placed in an ambulance, which then sped away with the siren blaring.

Dragon spotted a KSL-TV news crew doing a live report from on the street below him, so he turned on the TV to see what they were saying. The female reporter was nearly hyperventilating as she said, "Details are sketchy at this point, but apparently a bioterror attack was made today at Energy Solutions Arena. An anonymous source told us that a maintenance worker encountered an Asian man spreading some sort of toxic material throughout the building. When she confronted him, he attacked her and stuffed her in a closet before fleeing. She was severely beaten, but she was able to crawl from the closet and alert other workers about what happened."

Dragon shook his head. " I'm such a fool! I should've made sure she was dead."

The reporter continued, "Authorities have in their possession the canister the man had used, and it is being tested to see exactly what type of toxic material it contained. They are also examining surveillance footage may provide clues to the man's identity. Needless to say, all upcoming events are postponed until further notice so that bioterror teams can check the entire building."

A sharp pain shot through Dragon's head and down his arm. He wasn't sure if it was an aneurysm or a heart attack, but something had snapped inside of him.

He turned off the TV, gathered up his belongings, then tore up his ID cards before flushing them down the toilet. He then walked slowly down the stairway to the lobby, where he calmly checked out of his room. From there he proceeded across the street to a

TRAX train depot, where he joined several other passengers on the platform. They were all watching the activity surrounding the nearby arena. Suddenly several policemen exited the building and hurried toward the hotel where Dragon had been staying.

"Uh, when's the train supposed to arrive?" he asked a man standing next to him.

"It should be here any minute," the man said.

Dragon was so worried about being caught by the Americans—but he was more concerned about the response his countrymen would give if his connection to the toxin was discovered. His Chinese superiors would deny any knowledge of Dragon's plans, leaving him on his own to face a long prison sentence.

Within moments three policemen exited the hotel and began working their way to the TRAX station. The train was now making its way down the tracks. A ray of hope briefly filled Dragon's heart that he might escape, but deep down he knew it would only prolong the chase.

"I'm a disgrace," he said before stepping onto the tracks as the train approached. The train engineer had no chance to respond, and Dragon's life was over in an instant.

～

By that night the news had spread across the nation that a bioterror attack had taken place in Salt Lake City. Anyone who had been within two blocks of the arena was urged to go to a local hospital and be tested, although the doctors didn't dare to admit what they were looking for.

The problem was that the residue in the canister was a chemist's ultimate nightmare. As the results came through showing a variety of diseases, U.S. officials knew they weren't dealing with a lone homegrown terrorist. This mixture could only have been produced in one of the world's finest laboratories.

Once Jasmine Bradley's identity was released, she was hailed as a national hero. She was in quarantine at LDS Hospital, though, because she'd been in contact with the toxin. Doctors were anxious to see if she developed any illnesses, and she soon developed severe pneumonia. She passed away within a week, but not before she became a media darling for having saved thousands of people from a similar fate.

In all of the commotion, it took police a few days to make the connection between the Asian man killed by the TRAX train and the one described by Jasmine. Since Dragon's body didn't have any identification, the police sent his remains to the state medical examiner's office in hopes of finding out who he was, but he didn't have the chip, and his fingerprints didn't come up in any national databases.

However, officials had found the custodian clothes among Dragon's scattered belongings, and traces of the canister's toxic residue were found his lungs. Officials assured the nation that the TRAX suicide victim was indeed the perpetrator, and they proclaimed that this was an isolated incident.

❧

The Chinese leaders watched the news reports coming out of Salt Lake with some amusement. Yes, Dragon had failed to complete his assignment, but the media circus surrounding the attack was actually a blessing in disguise for the Coalition's plans. The media was keeping careful vigils on a dozen Energy Solutions Arena employees who were in varying degrees of sickness, as well as a well-known pro wrestler who had gone to the arena early that day, contracted the disease, and was now the face of the bioterror attack.

America's health officials had expanded their testing to include anyone who had been in Salt Lake that day, and they encouraged travelers to avoid passing through the state. Meanwhile, Dragon's partners Rain, Wind, and Fire had all succeeded spectacularly in their missions and were already out of the country, enjoying their financial rewards.

As the nation's health officials focused on keeping infected people from leaving or entering Salt Lake, the toxic microbes multiplied across the nation, spreading from New York, Los Angeles, and San Francisco like an invisible tidal wave. As they were passed from person to person—then through entire families—America's social fabric began to unravel from within.

CHAPTER 27

By late May, hospital emergency rooms throughout California and along the East Coast were packed with people complaining of severe flu symptoms. Interestingly, the U.S. doctors gave it the same name their Chinese counterparts did—the "Black Flu" because of the effect it had on people's skin. There were other symptoms emerging, such as white sores and bleeding from the mouth and ears, but it was the jarring sight of darkened bruised flesh that was causing a panic among the nation's citizens.

It was clear to U.S. health officials that this illness was the same one Jasmine Bradley had contracted at Energy Solutions Arena. They had never revealed photos of her body, but she'd been covered with dark splotches and sores by the time she passed away.

The president's cabinet met secretly on the Wednesday before Memorial Day, and as they listened to updated reports on the spread of the Black Flu, it became clear that the Salt Lake attack wasn't the origin of the illness. They realized other attacks had been successfully completed on both coasts. Something had to be done immediately or else the nation would be completely crippled by the illness. That afternoon the U.S. president appeared on TV in a special broadcast from the Oval Office.

"Good evening, my fellow Americans," the president said. "At this time, our country faces a major challenge even more destructive than the natural disasters we've recently faced. It's called the 'Black Flu.' Many of you in our larger cities are experiencing it firsthand within your homes and neighborhoods, while other areas aren't affected yet."

He cleared his throat and added, "Unfortunately, all indications are that the survival rate for this flu is terribly low. Our scientists are laboring day and night to come up with a vaccine to combat this illness, but we are still weeks away from achieving a satisfactory result. For this reason, I'm issuing an executive order that all domestic air travel cease immediately to halt the spread of this virus. We will also begin restricting travel across state lines."

The president paused, knowing the strong reaction this announcement would create across America. "This is a decision I haven't made lightly, because I know the impact it will have on folks across this land. However, this is a matter of national security. A series of checkpoints will be established throughout the nation to ensure that the virus is contained. Citizens who show symptoms of the illness should be treated with compassion, but they must be isolated to halt the spread of the disease."

The president then stared into directly into the camera. "I don't want this crisis to divide our nation, but I urge any communities that are not yet affected to create 'quarantine zones' so that this terrible illness won't infiltrate your neighborhoods as it plays itself out. I'm confident that as we work together to overcome this national trial, we'll emerge as a stronger nation."

⁂

In Chicago, Marie Shaw joined her co-workers around a TV in the lobby of Naples & Austin to watch the president's announcement. They looked at each other in shock afterward.

"What are we going to do?" Bianca asked in a panic. "I'll bet hundreds of infected people have already passed through O'Hare Airport, so it'll start spreading here quickly."

Gretchen emerged from her office, where she had also been watching the president's message. "Our option is quite simple," she said. "This is our home until the epidemic passes."

"What do you mean?" Marie asked.

"This office is where we'll stay," Gretchen said. "We need to act quickly to stock up on food and water, but otherwise we could live here comfortably for weeks—and even keep working on our projects."

Gretchen ordered all of the male employees to go down to the shopping mall on the building's lower floors and buy all the food they could. They returned an hour later with bags of food, but it wasn't nearly as much as they'd hoped.

"It's a madhouse down there," one man said, showing a torn shirt. "The president's message has sent everyone into a panic. We need to barricade ourselves in, because it won't be long before people start coming up here searching for food."

"I've got some food in my apartment," Marie said. "Can I go get it?"

All eyes turned to Gretchen, since about a dozen employees had condos in the building. After a moment she said, "Yes, that's a good idea, Marie. Everyone who lives in the building go retrieve anything useful. After you return, we'll block off the elevator door and the stairwells."

Within a few moments, Marie was in the elevator heading to her apartment. She entered her living room, and it struck her how meaningless all of her possessions now seemed. She went through the cupboards and the refrigerator, and soon she had three plastic bags filled with items.

Then she heard a voice that seemed to come from inside her.

"*Don't go back there.*"

Marie stopped in her tracks.

"*You'll die if you rejoin them. Leave this building.*"

Then Marie's mind was opened to a quick view of her future if she returned to the Naples & Austin office. The images were frightening and disturbing, and included her own violent death. It reminded her of a statement she'd once heard—"The average person is only a couple of layers away from being a savage."

Marie dropped to her knees, overwhelmed by what had just occurred, but she knew it was the Spirit talking to her. She hadn't necessarily listened to heavenly promptings very well during the past couple of years, but there was no denying it this time.

"Thank thee, Heavenly Father. I will leave."

Just then her cell phone rang. The caller ID showed Gretchen's number, so Marie let it go to voice mail. Once the call was completed, she listened to Gretchen's anxious message—"Marie, where are you? I talked to a friend who works in the mall, and things are getting even worse down there. So we're barricading the doors in fifteen minutes. Do you need help bringing your things? I'll send Vince down to help you. Return my call immediately."

Marie shuddered and rapidly filled a duffel bag with some granola bars, tuna, snacks, and a few bottles of water. She was terrified that her co-worker would show up any moment, but she quickly changed out of her business attire into a T-shirt, jeans, and sneakers.

She grabbed the duffel bag, slammed the door behind her, and hurried toward a nearby stairwell. It would be a long winding walk down, but she didn't dare use the elevator in case another employee happened to be on it.

As she entered the darkened stairwell, she heard Vince call her name from the hallway. She looked back over her shoulder and locked eyes with him briefly, then took off down the stairs. She had never moved so quickly.

Marie heard him enter the stairwell and shout, "Marie! Where are you going?"

"You can have everything in my apartment," she shouted back. "Just leave me alone."

Vince didn't respond, and she kept moving downward. The stairwell soon ended at the edge of the building's main lobby. She saw hundreds of people in a big commotion. She entered the lobby and ducked her head as she tried to plow her way through to the main entrance, but she kept getting jostled around. Suddenly a large man was in her face shouting, "The end has come! The end has come!"

Marie shoved past him and fought through the frantic crowd until she reached the street. There was only one place she'd felt close to heaven during her time in Chicago—the Smith Museum of Stained Glass Windows. She broke into a trot and headed in that direction, arriving 20 minutes later at Navy Pier.

Marie could hardly fathom that it had been less than a month since that peaceful Sunday afternoon she'd enjoyed on the pier. The area was once again filled with hundreds of people, but this time no one was leisurely walking along. Everyone looked agitated and nervous. Thankfully, they all seemed to be hurrying somewhere else. However, a woman ran by and snatched at Marie's backpack, nearly ripping it off her shoulder. Marie yanked it back and gave the woman a threatening look.

"Get out of here, you piece of white trash," Marie snarled, causing the woman to scamper away. Marie was happy to still have her backpack, but she was surprised at the primal venom that had come from her own mouth.

"How could one simple announcement cause all of this fear?" Marie thought Then it dawned on her that America had been teetering on this kind of chaos for quite a while. The president's announcement had simply unleashed this underlying tension. Now it was suddenly every man, woman, and child for themselves.

∽

Marie went directly to the museum, where an older woman was putting on a jacket near the front desk.

"Sorry, but we're about to close," the woman said.

Marie stepped inside and smiled politely. "I just want to look around for awhile."

"Are you crazy?" the woman asked. "Didn't you hear what the president said today?"

"I did, but I have nowhere else to go," Marie said. "I feel peaceful when I'm here."

The woman motioned dramatically at a display. "Well, I'm glad you like the place, but I've got to lock up. Scram!"

Marie just stood still. "Don't worry about me. Go ahead and

lock me in. I'll turn off the lights and shut the door behind me when I leave."

The woman stared at her in surprise, then threw her hands in the air. "Fine! Stay here if you want, but I've got to get home to my family."

"Thank you," Marie said. "I really appreciate this."

The woman merely gave her a strange look before rushing out the door. Once she was gone, Marie made sure the door was indeed locked, then she jammed a chair under the door knob and dragged a table in front of it. She suspected the woman wouldn't ever be back, and Marie didn't want any company.

Once the table was in place, she sank to her knees and prayed, "Heavenly Father, thank thee for helping me find safety. Help me to do thy will."

CHAPTER 28

Despite everything people heard on the news, Utah was actually one of the least affected areas in the nation. Dragon's failure to complete his mission—combined with the fact that people had been warned against traveling there—had kept the Black Flu to a minimum in the state. However, that didn't stop the rumor mill from operating at full strength.

In the days following the bioterror attack, the citizens of Utah endured a flurry of half-truths and misinformation. One rumor said everyone needed to go to the closest government building and take a pill that would help fight off the disease. Soon there were long lines forming around post offices and city halls, but no such announcement had ever been made.

Then came the word that the military was going to use helicopters to spray down the streets with a sanitizer. This prompted most people to stay inside for a day until it was clear that this was just another false story.

Church members who hadn't gone to the camps were particularly vulnerable to such stories. One rumor said the government was rounding up any remaining Mormons to hold them as ransom until the prophet turned himself in as a fugitive. That caused quite a stir, but no word came from Church officials about whether it was true. That was the most agonizing part for the Mormons still in the valleys—they were accustomed to at least hearing something from their leaders, but now the Church was silent.

Under these circumstances, the maintenance missionaries found many opportunities to assist people who were struggling to cope with how the world had changed. In Nathan's case, he had felt guided to walk to the Provo Temple. As he approached the area he saw dozens of families milling around on the lawn between the temple grounds and the Missionary Training Center. The temple was surrounded by fencing—just like all of the others—and the guards had been instructed to not let anyone inside.

There was an armed guard standing near the temple's west gate, and Nathan motioned for him to speak with him. As the man approached, Nathan quietly repeated the password to him. After Nathan said "Amen" the guard nodded and started to open the gate, but dozens of people in the crowd had been watching him and began moving toward them.

"It's okay," Nathan told the guard. "Leave it shut. I just felt prompted to come here. Who are all of these people?"

The guard shrugged. "They're members of the Church, but they're the ones who ignored the prophet's invitation. Now they're unemployed, hungry, out of money, and feeling desperate. There's not a lot I can do for them."

A lady tapped Nathan on the shoulder. "Excuse me, you seem to have connections with the guard. Can you convince him to let us in? There's food stored in the temple, right?"

Nathan looked at her swollen eyes. It was clear she had been sobbing heavily. It broke his heart, but he said, "Sorry, we can't let you in."

The lady dropped her head. "It's just that our world has fallen apart, and we know we made a mistake. Things just keep getting worse around here. Can't you please tell us where the rest of the members are?"

Nathan shook his head. "I really wish I could, but those camps are sealed off anyway. But maybe I can still help. Just a minute."

Nathan walked away from the group and offered a prayer in his heart about whether he should lead these families to a "blue camp." He knew one had been established in the Wallsburg Valley near Deer Creek Reservoir.

The Spirit confirmed his suggestion, and he returned to the

woman's side. "I know a safe place you can go. It's up Provo Canyon, and I'll lead you there."

The woman's face lit up, and she gave him a hug. "That would be wonderful!"

Word quickly spread that Nathan would lead a group to a camp, and by the end of the day they had walked a few miles before stopping along the Provo River near the Riverwoods shopping complex. They spent the night inside an abandoned store before beginning the hike through the canyon. It took the group three more days to reach the camp, which didn't compare at all to the "white camps" where the faithful Saints were, but the people were happy to be there. There were a few hundred people already at the camp, and they didn't look thrilled to add any newcomers, but at least Nathan had followed his prompting.

"Hopefully they'll find ways to get along," Nathan told himself as he hiked back down the canyon. He reached Orem two days later, and although he wanted to just curl up and go to sleep, the Spirit screamed at him to go to his father's house. When he arrived there, Garrett's car wasn't in the driveway and the house was dark. He knocked loudly, but there wasn't an answer.

"Vanessa! Denise!"

He peered through the windows, then finally gave up, unsure why he'd been prompted so strongly. Then as he was walking away, he heard a window open behind him.

"Nathan!"

It was Denise. She looked terrified. Nathan ran back to the house, and she opened the door and rushed into his arms.

"I'm so glad you're here," she said. "I wasn't sure what to do."

"What do you mean?"

"I think Mom and Dad are dead!"

The words literally jolted Nathan, and he peered past her into the house. "Where are they? In their bedroom?"

"No, not here. They went to Los Angeles the day before the bioterror attack to help my aunt move here after the earthquake. But Dad must've caught that new disease, because Mom said she had taken him to the hospital after he got those dark spots people get. The next day she called to say he wasn't doing very good and that she wasn't feeling well. Plus, she was worried with the new travel restrictions they wouldn't be able to come back anyway."

"When did you last talk to her?" Nathan asked.

"Three days ago. I've called and texted her lots of times since then, but she doesn't answer."

Nathan was still reeling from the news. "How come you didn't go with them?"

"I had all of my school finals that I couldn't miss, so I stayed home. They were only going to be gone a few days."

"This is terrible," Nathan said. "So you've been living here alone all this time?"

"Yes. I've just hidden away."

"I've got some friends who can help you," Nathan said. "Let's go see if they're home."

CHAPTER 29

Nathan and Denise walked over to the Shaws' home and found Carol tending her tomato plants alongside the house. She walked over to the sidewalk and greeted them.

"It's so good to see you," she said, giving Nathan a hug. "And you must be Nathan's sister Denise, right?"

Denise brightened, surprised that this woman already knew her name. "That's right."

Carol motioned back toward the house. "You're probably wondering why I care about my tomatoes when the world is falling apart around us, but it keeps my mind off things."

"We completely understand," Nathan said. "We've got things on our minds, too. Our parents went to Los Angeles to help some relatives, but we're afraid they've caught the Black Flu. We haven't heard from them in a couple of days."

"Oh, that's terrible," Carol said. "Is there anything I can do to help?"

Denise shifted a little. "Would it be possible for me to stay with you? I've been alone for a few days now, and it's a little scary."

"Absolutely," Carol said. "Let's go inside. Besides, Aaron wanted to talk to you, Nathan."

They found Aaron in the kitchen, and after sharing their news, Carol started helping Denise settle in. "You can stay in Marie's room."

"Is Marie your daughter?" Denise asked. "The girl Nathan really likes?"

"Yes, that's her," Carol said, winking at Nathan. "Hopefully

Marie will come home soon from Chicago, but I know she'd be happy to have you stay in her room. Let me show it to you."

As they moved down the hall, Aaron motioned to Nathan. "Let me show you the garden. The tomatoes are starting to get taller."

Nathan got the hint, and they moved outside to avoid being overheard by potential eavesdroppers. They began walking through the garden when Aaron turned to Nathan and said, "I've got some news about Marie. She left her apartment and abandoned her internship a few days ago. She seems to be hiding in a building along the shore of Lake Michigan."

The information took Nathan by surprise. "Hiding? What makes you think that?"

"Well, it's hard to pinpoint exactly what's she's doing," Aaron said. "At first I was afraid she'd been kidnapped, but she's definitely alone. No one else with a chip has entered that part of the building. She moves around enough that I know she's alive, but maybe she's got the Black Flu."

"Have you told Carol?" Nathan asked.

"I did share a few things with her, since Marie won't answer our phone calls. My feeling is that things got really bad there quickly after the president's announcement and so Marie took off. When we talked to her a few weeks ago, she mentioned a museum she had visited on Navy Pier, and it looks like she's now in that same location. I'm guessing she has barricaded herself in there."

"What can we do?" Nathan asked. "I'm willing to go there and find her."

"I knew you would say that, but it's terribly risky," Aaron said. "The government has been tracking a Chicago gang leader named Brix who has been operating in that part of the city, and it appears his followers are already looting stores and burning buildings near where Marie is. We're really worried it could turn into a civil war there within days."

Aaron looked at Nathan's anguished face and added, "Don't worry, Carol and I have made our peace that Marie might never come home."

"Well, I haven't," Nathan said fiercely. "My car is still in my dad's garage. I'll drive all day and all night if I have to."

Aaron looked Nathan straight in the eyes. "Are you that determined? Would it interfere with your Church assignment?"

Nathan shook his head. "Right now my only command is to follow the Spirit in helping the Saints who aren't in the camps yet. Marie certainly falls in that category."

Aaron couldn't help getting misty-eyed. "Okay, you've convinced me. Let me show you something that will make your trip a lot easier."

He pulled a gadget out of his pocket that looked like an iPhone, but a little thicker. He held it out to Nathan, who took it and examined it. "Is this a newfangled phone?"

Aaron lowered his voice. "No, it's a chip tracking device. The only people who have them so far are members of the CCA. I smuggled this one out last week. Thankfully this first model has a flaw—the government forgot to make the tracking device itself to be traceable, so no one will know you have it."

"I like that," Nathan said. "What exactly can it do?"

Aaron took the device back and touched the screen. "It has several functions, but there are two that will really help you. It can track an individual, and it also can detect when someone else with a chip is nearby. So you'll be able to keep track of Marie, but you'll also be able to check if anyone is following you."

"This is great, but didn't the president say the government is setting up checkpoints at the state borders?" Nathan asked. "How will I make it without getting caught?"

"If you stick to the back roads you'll be all right. The president's announcement came as a surprise to nearly everyone, and so they've hardly started implementing those programs. It was more of a scare tactic to make people stay in one place until they can get a handle on this disease."

"That's a relief, but something else just dawned on me," Nathan said. "My car gets great gas mileage, but I'll never make it that far. What should I do for fuel?"

Aaron pulled out his wallet and handed Nathan a stack of $20 bills. "Cash is still king, especially at the gas pump. The prices are getting crazy, but with no one traveling, the station owners will be happy to have a customer. Plus, I've got some five-gallon cans in the garage you can put in the trunk."

"Wonderful," Nathan said. "I'll get the house key from Denise and then bring my car over here."

Aaron started to get a little emotional again. "Thank you, Nathan. I was hoping you would come by soon. We're running short on time. This Black Flu has been bad on the nation, but there's something coming down the pipeline that is going to inflame things even more. They told us at work that the government is going to stop providing welfare and unemployment benefits soon."

"Oh boy. Don't they know what that will spark?"

"They do, but they don't seem to care. Their attitudes are so callous that they're actually looking forward to people killing each other in the streets. I've heard it referred to as a 'population decrease.' Then they expect things will settle down and we'll get the nation back on track."

"Whoa," Nathan said. "That's some pretty dark thinking."

"It is, but it's also reality," Aaron said. "Along those same lines, they also see the disease as a great way to balance the books on Medicare, Medicaid, and Social Security. They know there's going to be a temporary economic crunch because there won't be as much tax money coming in during the crisis, but then those entitlement programs will suddenly be in a lot better shape if millions of people are no longer on the rolls."

"That's barbaric," Nathan said. "But after what I've seen lately, it's not surprising. Even though there's still enough food to go around, people already seem eager to cut each other's throats."

Aaron nodded grimly. "That's exactly why we've got to get Marie out of Chicago."

"You get me started, and I'll find a way," Nathan said.

"We'll figure out a route for you before you leave. Staying on smaller highways will be your best bet, because for the most part there's nothing but a few rural towns and farmland out there. The government will be focusing on the cities first."

"How far is it to Chicago?" Nathan asked.

"It's about 1,500 miles from here, so you've got quite a drive ahead of you."

Nathan shrugged. "This is for Marie. It'll be worth it."

CHAPTER 30

Marie had been in the Stained Glass Windows Museum for four days when the power went out. Up to that point, she was actually enjoying her secluded hideaway. She'd found a stash of bottled water in a cupboard, and she was rationing the food supplies she'd brought with her.

The museum was essentially a long hallway with window displays positioned at various points, creating a walking tour. The only doorways were the entrance and the exit, and Marie had blocked them off the best she could. She felt somewhat safe, but she was prepared to hide in a secluded area behind a set of windows if someone broke in.

However, when the power went out, the whole atmosphere of the museum changed. Without the lights on, it felt eerie during the day, with only a meager amount of sunlight filtering in through some stained glass windows that were part of the outside wall. The night was much worse, and every sound coming from the pier made her heart race. She heard a steady wail of emergency sirens, and she figured the illness was likely hitting Chicago hard.

As she reached the one-week mark in the museum, she was essentially out of food. She had tried to resist eating her final granola bar, but she just couldn't help it. Finally late one night she couldn't take the solitude and starvation any longer. She slipped out the back entrance of the museum and was astounded at the mixture of sounds that filled her ears. The museum walls had effectively muted the city noise, but now the sirens could be heard clearly, as well as sporadic rounds of gunfire.

The biggest surprise was that she couldn't see anyone walking along the pier. It had always been bustling with people, but now it was dark and abandoned. The stars blazed above her, the first time she'd noticed them since leaving Utah. She stepped out onto the pier far enough to get a better look at the darkened city and was shocked to see flames engulfing three separate skyscrapers along the Magnificent Mile.

"Hey! What are you doing?" a man called out as he shined a flashlight on her. "Get over here! Don't you know the mayor declared a mandatory curfew in this area?"

The man was about hundred yards away, and Marie immediately bolted back toward the museum. She quietly shut the door, then barricaded it again. She listened intently for the man to approach, but he apparently didn't know where she'd gone.

She clutched her stomach as it rumbled for the hundredth time that day. "Heavenly Father, am I supposed to just die here?"

As Marie prayed for help, Nathan was traveling Highway 20 in the middle of Iowa. He'd been driving non-stop for three days, other than parking on empty dirt roads a couple of times to catch some sleep. Overall, the traffic had been minimal, and it was clear that the president's order about crossing state lines was being taken seriously.

The route Aaron had helped Nathan create would keep him off the main freeways unless absolutely necessary. He had traveled to Vernal first, and then crossed into Wyoming without seeing a checkpoint. He'd headed north to Casper, where he reached Highway 20 and crossed into Nebraska and then Iowa without any trouble. He'd stopped at a gas station in each state, and each time his cash was eagerly accepted.

As Nathan passed through Dubuque, Iowa, he pulled into a Wal-Mart parking lot. This was the one stretch of highway where he and Aaron were unsure what to do. Dubuque was on the western bank of the Mississippi River, and it was also the point where the borders of Wisconsin, Illinois, and Iowa touched. So there was a very strong chance a federal checkpoint would be in place at the bridge across the river. Dubuque was about 180 miles from Chicago, so Nathan hated to abandon the car this far from his goal, but he knew he'd never be allowed to drive across the bridge into Illinois.

As he sat in the parking lot, he pulled out the chip-tracking device. Aaron had given him a thorough lesson about it before he'd left Utah, and it had been surprisingly simple to figure out. He turned the device on and immediately checked on Marie's status. She was still in the same location she'd been for a week. She wasn't moving, but Nathan hoped she was just sleeping.

He then switched it to the feature that would pick up chip signals within 200 yards. He pointed it at the Wal-Mart store, and only about a dozen chips were identified. He scrolled through the names and hometowns of the people inside the store, but they were all Iowans who likely weren't heading east.

Nathan was actually surprised the store was even open. From what he'd seen during his drive across the country, most stores were now empty. Desperate shoppers had emptied the shelves within a couple of days after the president's announcement, and the trucking industry had essentially stopped making deliveries. He'd seen dozens of 18-wheelers parked in truck stops along the way, but he hadn't actually seen one traveling down the road since he left Wyoming.

As Nathan pondered his options, a nice sedan with Illinois license plates pulled up across from him. Two women jumped out—a blonde and a brunette—and they rushed into the store as if they really needed to go to the restroom. Nathan pointed the device at them and saw they were from Chicago.

An idea hatched in his mind while the women were in the store, but it seemed crazy, so he took a moment to pray about it. Within seconds he got a strong confirmation that it was the right decision to make.

"Okay, Lord," he thought. "This is out of my hands now."

When the women returned, Nathan got out of the car and approached them slowly. "Hello there," he said. "Are you two on your way to Illinois?"

The women looked at him cautiously before the blonde replied, "We hope, but we don't know if they'll let us cross the bridge. We both work in Chicago as nurses, though, so maybe they'll let us through. Why?"

"Oh, I just have a friend I'm trying to reach there, but there's no way they're going to let me through with my Utah license plates. Is there any chance I could catch a ride with you?"

The brunette looked skeptical. "Are you a Mormon?"

"Yes, I am."

She shook her head. "Then they'd never let us across with you in the car."

"They wouldn't even need to know I was there," Nathan said. "I can hide in the car trunk if you want."

The brunette rolled her eyes. "That would make things even worse. They'd track your chip in an instant."

"Uh, I don't have a chip. We'd be fine."

Both women did a double-take.

"That's strange," the blonde said. "Who are you?"

"That doesn't matter. Anyway, if I can just ride in your trunk to Chicago, I'll give you $100 when we get there. I'm actually trying to get to Navy Pier."

To make his point, he pulled the $20 bills from his pocket. The women looked at each other. The money had caught their attention. "We can get you within a couple miles of Navy Pier—if you make it $100 each."

Nathan frowned. Aaron had given him $500, and he had about $300 left. Finally he said, "It's a deal."

He got his backpack out of the car and then locked the door out of habit, although he was quite sure he'd never see it again. Then he put his life into the hands of two questionable strangers as he climbed into their trunk and they slammed it shut.

Ten minutes later, the car pulled up to the checkpoint at the bridge across the Mississippi River. Nathan listened intently as the women charmed the guard and said they were desperately needed in Chicago to help take care of Black Flu victims.

"Hold out your hands," the guard said.

Nathan heard the beeping of a chip-scanner, then the guard asked someone nearby, "What do you think? Their chips verify their story."

There was a muffled conversation, then the guard said, "Drive on. Go save some lives."

"Thank you so much," the blonde said as she hit the gas. Soon they were across the bridge into Illinois, and the women started playing a hip-hop music CD. The hours passed, and he prayed the women would hold up their part of the bargain. After a while Nathan remembered the chip-detector also had a GPS system. He switched to that mode and was relieved to see they were within a few miles of Chicago.

The music CD finally ended for the third time, and Nathan could hear snippets of the women's conversation. He was shocked to hear that they planned to pull a gun on him and threaten to turn him in for "chip non-compliance" if he didn't give them all of his money and possessions. They suddenly noticed the CD had stopped, and he heard one of them ask, "Do you think he's been listening to us?"

Then the music started playing again. Nathan began to search frantically for a handle to release the trunk from the inside, and thankfully the car had one. They soon left the freeway, and the car began stopping occasionally at intersections. They were still moving in the general direction of Navy Pier, so he planned to stay in the trunk a little while longer, but then the Spirit said clearly, "*Get out at the next stop.*"

As the car began to brake, Nathan pulled the handle. The trunk popped open, and he leaped out and took off running down a side street. The car went about 50 feet before the women noticed the trunk lid was up, and by then Nathan was long gone.

⁘

The next few minutes were among the most frightening of Nathan's life. He stayed in the middle of the street, which was only safe because the entire city was dark except for skyscrapers burning in the distance. He heard a lot of shouting inside many of the buildings that he passed, and he sensed families were beginning to collapse under the stress of the past few days.

He paused for a moment and set the chip-detector so that it treated Marie's chip like a geocache—giving him the remaining distance and direction to reach her. The device was designed for evil purposes, but it had been such a blessing in helping him on the journey.

Two blocks later he felt prompted to switch the device to the chip-detector mode, and he was stunned to see three people were about 30 yards behind him and getting closer. He pulled his handgun out of his pocket and whirled.

"Run the other way or I'll blow your heads off," he shouted.

His pursuers stopped in their tracks. One called out, "Hey, take it easy, man. We're not going to hurt you."

"I'm serious," Nathan said.

Another man laughed. "He's bluffing. The feds took away all of the guns. Let's get him. Brix would love to have another white boy to kick around."

The trio started moving forward, and Nathan didn't hesitate to pull the trigger. As the shot rang out, one of the men fell to the pavement, crying in agony. "Help me. I'm bleeding!"

Nathan instantly sprinted down the street for the next six blocks. At last he spotted what looked like the top of a Ferris Wheel. It had to be Navy Pier. He checked the device again and was thrilled to see he was within 200 yards of Marie. He soon reached the side of a building, and Marie was now only ten yards from him.

"She's got to be just inside," he thought as he searched frantically for a way in. He moved along the side of the building until he found a door. It was locked, and he tried to kick it in. It gave way, but something else was blocking it.

"Marie!" he called out. "It's me, Nathan! Are you there, Marie?"

❧

Marie was awakened from a restless sleep by a loud crash. Someone was trying to break in! She rushed to her hiding place behind one of the stained glass displays, but then she heard a faint voice. "Marie! Marie! Let me in!"

She knew that voice. Could it possibly be true?

She cautiously approached the door. "Nathan?"

"Yes! Oh, Marie! I'm so glad you're alive!"

She was almost too weak to move the desk that was blocking the door, but she moved it just enough that Nathan could squeeze inside. He leaped over the desk and they found each other in the dark. He took her in his arms, then kissed her gently.

She hugged him tightly, still struggling to comprehend what was happening. "How did you get here?"

"A series of miracles. The important thing is we're together."

He kissed her again, and Marie felt safe for the first time in months. They hugged tightly, and Nathan whispered, "Everything is going to be all right."

A Crippled Nation

The next morning, Nathan and Marie began planning their escape from Chicago, but their options were even more limited than they imagined.

The nation was falling apart economically, food shortages were developing, and most medicines were running out. Although there were still a few peaceful rural areas left in America, the nation's cities were falling prey to a "survival of the fittest" mentality that was causing fear and anger among the citizens.

In order to stabilize the nation, the U.S. president had made a secret request to the United Nations, arranging for them to send in "peacemakers" to help quell the growing unrest.

Join Nathan and Marie as they seek to rejoin the Saints when the *Times of Turmoil* series continues in *Book Two: Martial Law.*

ABOUT THE AUTHOR

Chad Daybell has written two dozen books for the LDS market. He is best known for his popular *Standing in Holy Places* series, as well as his non-fiction books for youth, including *The Aaronic Priesthood* and *The Youth of Zion*. He and his wife Tammy also created the *Tiny Talks* series for Primary children.

Chad has worked in the publishing business for the past three decades. He is currently the president of Spring Creek Book Company. Visit **www.springcreekbooks.com** to see the company's lineup of titles.

Learn about Chad and the upcoming volumes in the *Times of Turmoil* series at his personal website **www.cdaybell.com**.